The Phantom's Gold

ERIC MURPHY

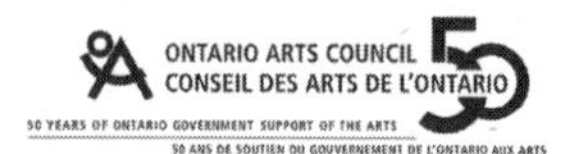

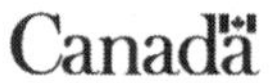

The publisher gratefully acknowledges the support of the Canada Council for the Arts and the Ontario Arts Council for its publishing program. We acknowledge the financial support of the Government of Canada through the Canada Book Fund (CBF) for our publishing activities, and the Government of Ontario through the Ontario Media Development Corporation, an agency of the Ontario Ministry of Culture, and the Ontario Book Publishing Tax Credit Program.

LIBRARY AND ARCHIVES CANADA CATALOGUING IN PUBLICATION

Murphy, Eric, 1952–
The phantom's gold / Eric Murphy.

Issued also in electronic formats.
ISBN 978-1-77086-266-1

I. Title.

PS8626.U754P53 2013 JC813'.6 C2013-900483-1

Front and back cover: Nick Craine
Interior text design: Tannice Goddard, Soul Oasis Networking

Printed and bound in Canada.
Manufactured by Friesens in Winnipeg, Manitoba, Canada in April, 2013.

This book is printed on 100% post-consumer waste recycled paper.

DANCING CAT BOOKS
An imprint of Cormorant Books Inc.
390 Steelcase Road East, Markham, Ontario, L3R 1G2
www.dancingcatbooks.com
www.cormorantbooks.com

The Phantom's Gold

Chapter One

A Cry for Help

Sou'wester: wide-brimmed, waterproof hat used during storms

William was shaken awake and knew something bad was happening. The pickup his father was driving pounded down the moonlit embankment. His father was slumped over the steering wheel and his chest was blaring the horn. They flew over the retaining wall.

For that moment of weightlessness he thought he was still asleep and dreaming. The headlights bounced off the ocean's surface till they ploughed into the oncoming waves. His seatbelt jerked him in place. Water snaked in around his calves.

His chest hurt, but it was all that dark water that made William scream, "Dad!"

Waves reached over the hood, hissing steam off the motor. His dad's sou'wester washed over his knees. His father hung over the steering wheel, his face twisted towards him. Fear coated William's tongue with the taste of copper. He reached for his dad just as the headlights' spill died underwater. The incoming tide rode higher up the windshield. It flooded the cab to his chest. They had to get out or drown.

"Dad!" he hollered, shaking his father. "The seatbelt's stuck. Dad, wake up! I need your knife. The seat belt —" Freezing water gripped his neck and constricted his chest, making it hard to breathe. He could feel the cold draining the strength from his fingers. He pawed at his father's pants pocket, caught the lanyard, and pulled the rigging knife free. Brine washed over his mouth. He held his breath. He willed his shaking hands to pry the stubby blade open. It nicked his thumb. He winced as he slashed his seatbelt till it was severed. He floated out of his seat and his head touched the roof.

He pulled his father's seatbelt and sliced at it. Lungs burning, he spun around to the small air pocket trapped against the roof and sucked in air. "Dad, you're too big. I can't get you out." His dad hadn't moved. His eyes and mouth were frozen open.

He pushed the door. It wouldn't open. Desperate for air, he pulled himself through the open window. His father's rain hat floated out after him. He reached for the roof, which was still above the surface, dropping his whalebone-handled knife. He pulled himself onto the roof and pounded, yelling, "Dad, Dad, Dad. Get out. Please, get out, please."

The last of the air burst out of the truck in a death rattle. A wave knocked William clear of the hood and into the icy water, where he half-floated, half-swam for shore. He stared back for a sign of life he knew wouldn't come.

The tide pummelled him to the slippery shore, where he lay shivering. The waves *clickety-clacked* small beach stones with indifference to one more life, one more death.

They had come to Nova Scotia for his birthday. He would stay for a funeral.

"Dad!" His cry woke him up like it always did. He gasped for air, relieved to see he was in his bed, back in Toronto. His hands clutched the bottom sheet. It had come away from the mattress again. His alarm clock read 11:02. He staggered to his bedroom window and inhaled the warm night air. The accident was a year old but his memory of it was still raw.

He looked out to the moonlit carport. That's where his dad used to park the truck with its blue and red Jack McCoy Sails logo. Where was the truck now? he wondered. What had they done with it in the year since the accident? Had somebody tried to fix it, to repair the slashed seatbelts?

That night in Nova Scotia he had been in shock and barely remembered anything but the flashing lights. So many of them flashing around him from the police, the ambulance, and the fire truck.

The ambulance attendants had wrapped him in blankets. They wanted him to stay inside. William wanted to see the divers bring his father out, to see them tow the truck out of the ocean. He remembered an RCMP officer scolding the ambulance driver for letting him watch. Why? He needed to see his father's body and the truck. He needed to believe it had actually happened. That it wasn't just a nightmare.

The officer had ordered another police officer to take him to his grandparents' place, a half-hour drive away just outside Lunenburg. To have come so close to his grandparents' house and not to have made it was unfair. He stopped shaking and fell asleep in the police car. He never saw his father being pulled out of the water. The next time he saw him, he was in a coffin. He looked like he did when he slept on the couch on Sunday afternoons. Except this time he wore a suit and his chest didn't go up and down no matter how long William stared and hoped.

His father had been so proud of that truck. Like everything else it was probably ruined. His mom would know but he couldn't ask her. All his questions about his dad and the accident made her cry. After a while he stopped asking her questions.

He looked from the carport to the newly staked for-sale sign on the lawn. Yesterday a man from the real estate company had pounded that sign into the lawn. His mom said selling the house would help put the bad memories behind them. William didn't think so.

He heard her turn down the radio. She had heard him yell and would be up in a moment. His nightmares weren't as frequent, and she wasn't as quick to respond, but she always came up. The anniversary of his father's death was a few days away. Maybe that's what stirred up the nightmare. Or maybe it was the fear of selling the house.

He looked back out at the carport and wondered why his memories of the truck and his father had begun to fade. He shook his head with annoyance, then stared at his hands to remember the exact location of his father's calluses, but he couldn't be sure. In the last few years he hadn't held his father's hands as much as he used to, say, when crossing the street, but there had been something reassuring about their size. The calluses had said he was a man who made things. No more.

"Will, are you all right?" called his mother from the living room.

"Yeah, I'm okay, Mom. Just, you know …," he answered.

Back in Toronto after the funeral, his school had made him visit with a grief counsellor. He asked him the questions he couldn't ask his mother. His father had once told him he had a special place in his heart for William. What became of that special place now that he was dead? Did his father still think of him now that he was dead? Did all that die in the truck too?

The counsellor had asked William if he believed in life after death, if his family was religious. They didn't go to church on Sundays and they didn't talk about God or anything like that. The counsellor asked William what he thought happened when a person died. He answered that if he knew the answer he wouldn't have asked the counsellor, would he? The man stammered and cleaned his glasses. William had other questions that the counsellor couldn't answer. He still had questions.

Why hadn't his dad cared enough about his family to take better care of his health? Why didn't he know his death made them cry, gave him nightmares?

He got back into bed a moment before his mother knocked on his door.

She sat at the edge of his bed and patted his leg through the sheet. It was hot for early June. He couldn't stand anything more than a sheet.

"It wasn't so bad this time," he lied.

"You're sure?" He nodded. "Well, if you're all right, I have to get back downstairs, okay?"

"Is somebody here?"

"Brad just dropped in." She stood to go and he scowled. "I wish you wouldn't make that face when I mention his name."

"He's a fake."

"It's not nice to say things like that about him. He likes you. He even takes you out to watch the Blue Jays, he —"

"He's a fake, Mom. He smiles and puts his arm around me when you're there. But as soon as you're out of sight, he, like, just gets all cold and weird. He's a fake."

"I think we'll all feel better after we move. Even Brad thinks —"

"I don't care what he thinks. And I don't want to move. "

His mom's shoulders sagged. She sighed and tucked in the corners of his twisted bottom sheet. "This is one thing you're just going to have to do. We have to get on with our lives. It's important."

"Isn't that just running away?"

"All our tears haven't helped us find your father. I'm just … trying to find us."

"Me too. That's why I think we should attend the memorial with Granddad —"

She shook her head no. "Sometimes a person can care too much. Drown in all that caring —"

"I know about drowning," he replied. "But how is running away —"

She stood and smoothed out her skirt to indicate she was through with the subject. Her voice had gone flat like it did when the subject was too painful for her to be present. "Anyway, you're going camping with Saif and his dad tomorrow, and that'll be nice. And then we'll look at some new houses, and Brad says he'll help. Now, sleep tight. Don't let the bedbugs bite." She blew him a kiss.

He listened to her footsteps pad down the stairs. Then he heard that fake laugh that Brad did when he pretended everything was okay. William reached for the slippers his father used to put under the bed for him. They hadn't been there for a year now. He still looked.

He crossed the room, tiptoed to the landing, and sat to eavesdrop. He heard a cork pop and his mom's surprised, "Oh." He snuck down two steps. He could hear better and see some of the living room from the mirror on the stairwell.

Brad handed his mother a glass of wine. She rarely drank during the week and especially not this late. Brad raised his glass to make a toast: "To a new start and a better year. And to the most courageous and beautiful woman I've ever known."

His mother wrung her hands. She did that when things got awkward. Brad pulled a small case from his jacket and opened it. He was offering his mother a thin, glittering bracelet. "I wanted you to have this. It's been in our family for ages. Can't think of anybody who deserves it more."

"Oh, Brad, I don't know what to say."

"You know what they say, 'sweets for the sweets and diamonds for a diamond.'" He placed the bracelet on the mantle. It glittered.

William almost choked at the thought of his mother accepting jewellery from Brad.

No, no, he thought to himself. Say no. Say no. Refuse the bracelet. He bolted back to his bed and covered his head with his pillow. It stood to reason that a wedding ring would be next. That would change his life for the worse.

His father had warned him, "Invite the sun, expect a storm." He hadn't expected the storm that had become his life. His father's death had left him feeling like an outsider. His friends at school acted strange, as though death was contagious. One kid asked him if he was going to die, too. Then a bunch of them had run off laughing. Saif, his only real friend, stayed, his arm around him. "They're just stupid."

He didn't feel like he belonged with his classmates anymore or even in the neighbourhood. Before his dad's death, on Wednesdays his mom went to the gym. He and his dad went to the pub. They had dinner and a game of Scrabble. Everybody waved and clapped him on the back. Dylan, the barkeep, had the same joke when they walked in: "Two Guinnesses?"

William always ordered ginger beer. His dad had a Guinness. It was fun. Being a regular and having a regular life had died with his dad. He ventured to the pub a few weeks after the funeral, half hoping his dad would be there. He wasn't. It was awkward. Some looked away or couldn't wait to walk away. Some were polite. They asked how his mother was doing. He said she cried a lot. They got quiet or remembered an important call they had to make. Maybe it was just him. Maybe he wasn't comfortable around them because his dad wasn't there. Maybe because he wasn't a regular anymore.

Their home had been the last safe place, a comfortable place where he was a regular. Now his mother was going to sell their house and his safety zone. Brad's friendship with his mother was going to make William even more of an outsider. He got that dizzy feeling. The world was moving away from him. His mom moved towards Brad. If one adult could abandon you, so could another. Being all alone was dark and frightening.

He turned on the light and tried to read *Treasure Island*. He couldn't focus. He looked around his room for something to stop this sinking feeling. The light reached across his desk. It lit a card his grandparents had sent early, for his thirteenth birthday.

William picked it up. Inside he read his grandmother's inscription: "Happy Birthday to our Grandson, Willy-boy. We hope your thirteenth birthday will make us lucky enough to see you soon. It's been too long." She had signed it, "Granny and Granddad."

Inside was a photo of his father's parents. Mary and Daniel McCoy were two healthy and energetic people. They smiled in front of a rhododendron bush that burst purple flowers all around them. His grandmother's elegant grey hair, turquoise pendant earrings, and beaming smile still held something of the glamour girl she must have once been. She had retired as a schoolteacher five years ago. His father had said she was an awesome Scrabble player.

Anchored behind her was his grandfather in a checkered shirt looking strong more from shoulder width than height. His father had said Daniel McCoy's faint smile was one that belonged to a confident man. One who'd earned the right for his friends to call him the Rock. It was a face, his dad said, that invited friends to shelter behind him in case of gale, gun, or grief. That's what William needed right now: a big, safe, solid rock to shelter behind.

Chapter Two

Ghost Boats

Cockpit: the steering area nearer the stern of a smaller vessel

In the morning he woke and again looked at the picture of his grandparents standing by their house overlooking the ocean. He remembered the swing at the back of the house. He'd spent hours on it while the adults cooked meals, tended the garden, and laughed. If he swung really hard he could see over the hedge to his grandfather's sailboat bobbing on the glittering ocean. Then he knew what he was going to do. His grandparents smiled. They were happy. They were normal. He would run away to his grandparents in Nova Scotia and be a regular again in the place he and his father had tried to get to last summer.

There'd been an argument between his mother and his grandfather following his father's death. He didn't know what it involved. He knew not to ask. It was one of those questions that upset his mother. All that mattered to William was that it didn't involve him. It was obvious from his grandmother's note that they wanted to see him.

He tapped his computer back to life. He Googled "buses to Lunenburg." He looked up the times, connections, and cost. He opened his piggy bank and counted out the money he had there.

He would stop at the bank machine to take out all the money from his birthdays and Christmases and what he hadn't used from his allowance. He had enough money for the bus — just enough.

But how could he make sure he got there before his mom knew he had run away?

He waited till she left for work. He opened the little book with important phone numbers. He found Saif's dad's cell number and dialled it.

"Oh, hi, Mr. Assad. It's William McCoy. I was calling to say that I won't be able to go camping with you this weekend after all because I'm gonna help my mother clean up some of my dad's stuff ... Yes, a year already ... Yes, I'll miss you too." Most of this was true.

He erased the "seven" from the number he had just dialled. Copying his mother's handwriting, he pencilled in a "nine." If his mother called Mr. Assad, she'd get a wrong number. This would buy him time. He jammed the lunch his mom had made for him in the top pouch of his knapsack.

He took Brad's diamond bracelet from the mantle, wrapped it in tissue, and pocketed it. He never stole from his mother. This was different. She needed to be saved from Brad. He locked the door behind him and headed to the terminal.

The terminal would get busier as Friday wore into the weekend. He had been to the terminal a few times with Saif and his older brother when they had taken a bus to Saif's family cottage. There were three or four queues of people waiting outside for their buses to arrive. Without Saif's older brother to keep an eye on him, he made a point of being more alert.

As he walked into the bus terminal he saw a baby drop its milk bottle. He picked it up from under the seat where it had rolled and gave it to the mother. She thanked him.

When the man at the ticket wicket asked him if he was travelling alone, he lied and said he was travelling with his mom and little sister. Where were they? asked the man. He needed a mother. He got the idea to turn and wave to the woman with the baby. When she smiled and waved back, the man at the ticket counter didn't ask any more questions.

When he got on the bus, he thought it looked like a giant bug. Its rear-view mirrors stuck out like an ant's antennae. The comfortable seats and washroom at the back made his day-and-a-half trip bearable. They played movies but he couldn't afford to buy earphones to hear them. Instead he got halfway through Treasure Island, which was now face-down on the seat next to him. The rocking of the bus and the thrumming of its diesel engine made him sleepy.

His first glimpse of the ocean was near Saint-Jean-Port-Joli in Québec. It was strange to think that he'd been such a good swimmer before the crash. Now he panicked when he came close to big bodies of water. His hands got sweaty and he stole a glance at the driver. He looked in control. So had his dad before he crashed his pickup.

William had really liked that truck. It always drew admiring comments from teachers and classmates when his dad dropped him off at school.

The 1948 Chevrolet pickup had soft, round lines. His dad had rebuilt it: a new interior, a V-6, and chromed hubcaps on white-walled radial tires. His dad's business logo, Jack McCoy Sails, was stencilled on both doors in his telltale blue and red colours. Nobody had a truck like that.

The sound system made even the smallest sounds stand out. William often picked Toots and the Maytals because they both liked reggae. There had even been a chorus of the old song from his childhood, "Down by the Bay," where the whale had a polka dot tail. His father had stretched it with new sightings. They included a bear in a chair, eels with heels, and pigs with wigs down by the bay where the watermelons grow. He hadn't had a belly laugh like that since his father's death.

That night of the accident, William had pulled the lanyard attached to the bone-handled rigging knife in his dad's pocket. It had a big spike called a marlinspike at one end. You used it to unscrew the pin in a shackle. William thought shackles looked like a horseshoe with a pin that locked it in various spots on a boat when something needed to be secured in place. He knew the spike was also used to pry open strands of rope when splicing one rope to another or onto itself in a strong loop. His father was skilled enough to do that. Those capable hands had provided a sense of security that had died that night.

William had unfolded the stubby blade and cut up their last apple, half for each of them. His dad growled before snapping up the segments, nibbling on William's fingers like some fruit-eating animal. William McCoy was embedded in gold inlay on the knife's handle. It had been his great-grandfather's knife. He had wiped the knife clean of apple juice, closed it on itself, and slipped it back into his dad's pocket. His dad had leaned in and kissed William's forehead.

They had talked about swimming out to the island in front of his grandfather's property and maybe getting permission to drive the Funmobile, his grandfather's van, on their land. Maybe he'd do it this year.

They had talked about sailing. It was strange that the son of a sailmaker didn't know how to sail. But William's dad was too rushed when trying out sails to bring a young son with him. He explained how he couldn't watch the shape of the sail, how it performed, and watch out for him at the same time. All that was supposed to change last year. William was going to learn to sail from his granddad, a master sailor. Then he and his father would crew for him in the annual race.

He had one clear memory of his grandfather sailing. He was maybe five years old. His grandfather swung him from the dock to the cockpit with one arm. The sail had been so smooth, William had fallen asleep.

They had talked a lot about his grandfather during the ride to Nova Scotia. Then William had laid his head against his dad's shoulder, sandwiched his big right hand between both of his own, and closed his eyes. He remembered feeling the calluses on the hands that cut, stitched, and hoisted so many beautiful sails, providing his clients with a product that usually exceeded their skill level. His mother called them his artist's hands.

If only William hadn't fallen asleep he might have been able to prevent the accident.

Best to think of the future. From his backpack he pulled out the dog-eared birthday card. The cover showed a pen-and-ink drawing of his grandfather's old-style shop called D & E Sailmakers. The shop's display window held a sailing trophy with a bronze schooner on top. They were supposed to race for that trophy last year.

He switched buses in Fredericton. He was nervous because he didn't know this terminal. He made a point of refilling his water bottle and stood in line at the gate long before his bus was scheduled to leave just to be sure he didn't miss it. He was about to ask the woman who stood behind him, to confirm that he was in the right line, when he saw that the ticket sticking out of her book read "Halifax." With just some coins left in his pocket he couldn't afford to get on the wrong bus.

Roadwork forced a short detour by the ocean before getting back to the Trans-Canada Highway. He scanned the Atlantic. It surged its high tide into the Bay of Fundy. William shivered at the memory of nearly being dragged out to sea. There was nothing out his window right now but darkness punctuated by shafts of moonlight. It reminded him of that night.

He fought back the memory of black sea water knocking him off the cab of the truck. He'd reached shore and clung to the edge of a rock, and the bullying tide had retreated with a hiss. He had escaped the foamy claws that tried to pull him back under.

The bus was miles away from the crash site, but the ocean that filled his bus window was the one from which they'd dragged his father's dead body. Some kind of shadow seemed to follow the bus along the water. William was too tired to give it much thought. He sat deeper in his seat. He closed his eyes and leaned against the bus window.

Whoosh! Lightning reached across the sky like a white crack zigzagging through black glass. Then, like in a horror movie, a second flash of lightning illuminated the shape of a forty-foot schooner sailing alongside the bus. He jerked his hands up and stared through splayed fingers.

The boat with the red jib sliced through one of the moonbeams. It flooded the cockpit with light. There was no one at the helm. Then a figure appeared in the cockpit. He laid a casual arm on the wheel. He was a big man, and William guessed he was about his grandfather's age. He wore an old-style rain slicker and fedora.

The look on his face as he stared at William was all business, right here, right now. It sent a chill down William's back. A snap of the man's hand magically filled the sails with wind. The schooner surged ahead. Spray burst from her bow. On the stern of the boat William read the name *Fathom*.

William blinked and peered out to the ocean: just rain *tick, tick, ticking* against the window like his mother's acrylic fingernails on the kitchen table when she brooded. He pulled his jacket tighter against the chill of a bad dream. Could he have slept with his eyes open?

Sheets of water splashed the window. Lightning pitchforked across the sky. Thunder double-boomed through the night like cannon fire from a distant battle. He felt alone and a long way from home. That would all change when he got to his grandparents.

Chapter Three

Cook Stop

Sloop: single-masted sailboat

The sun reflected off the puddles from last night's rain. William read the sign "Welcome to Lunenburg" through sleep-filled eyes. The bus pulled up to the Bluenose Lodge. He staggered off stiff, dragging his backpack.

Sleeping in fits and starts on buses wasn't the same as lying in his own bed. He stretched his back. The thought of his mother so far away rooted him to the spot. He was angry with her because of Brad and because she was selling the house. That just made the sadness ache more.

He hoisted his backpack onto his shoulders and headed towards the main street.

Lunenburg's old houses lent it the feel of a small town nestled in the past. It seemed familiar. Yet William was aware he'd forgotten much about the summers he'd spent here as a child. Last year's visit was the first one in four years. And it didn't count.

Most of the houses and buildings were clapboard. His grandfather's was like that. It was a style popular in the Maritimes and New England. Dwellings were clad in horizontal wooden boards that overlapped to seal their interiors from the rain and wind of coastal towns. Some houses were ornate, with bay windows or turret-like windows at the corners. These were probably owned by the wealthier colonists.

Even the simpler houses had interesting architecture, like a triangular structure over the door or a tiny bit of gingerbreading. He knew it was a well-planned British colonial town, and it did feel like he was time travelling as he walked down the street. William saw a few houses had the "Lunenburg bump," the five-sided Scottish dormer. His dad would often say of William's mother that when she was pregnant with him, she had looked as cute as a Lunenburg bump.

There were also a number of houses with what he knew was called a "widow's walk" — a top-floor walkway with a railing from which wives would look out to sea after a storm to see if their husbands were coming back. When it came to looking, William's mom had stopped. Their private storm still raged.

Seagulls wheeled and mewled overhead. They screeched so loudly they drowned out all other sound, then stopped and looped about looking for scraps floating in the harbour. Music filled the air. Standing by the government wharf was a musician playing guitar and singing a sad song. One of the nearby restaurants had a banner advertising the Lunenburg Music Festival.

William listened to the impromptu concert as he kept walking. The singer's ponytail, blond turning to grey, swayed over his shoulders. He smiled at William. His fingers flew up and down the mother-of-pearl inlaid guitar neck that flashed in the morning sun.

He wanted to ask directions but chose not to interrupt. His dad would have liked the lyrics.

Hey Nova Scotia,
How come you're calling out so loud?

Hey Nova Scotia,
I should have known that you'd be lost in the crowd.
Three Fathom Harbour, I hear you
Singing your mariner's songs,
The same songs the fishermen sing
From Lunenburg up to Lawrencetown.

William turned his head to the right and spotted a figure painting on the wharf. The painter was only visible because of a narrow gap between a wharf building and a parked van. What was on his easel? The man washed and placed his brushes in a wooden painter's case.

The painting was of a race in the harbour. Two sailboats heeled so far over, their rails were underwater. The lead boat, *Wave Goodbye*, was an elegant sloop. She edged her way past the two-masted schooner whose name was *Mary*.

William turned to the harbour. The blustery painting was a sharp contrast to the placid scene on the water. A faint breeze turned the real *Wave Goodbye*, which was sitting on the ocean's smooth surface. It barely stirred its yellow and green pennant. A gust rustled William's hair in greeting.

The painter's name, stencilled on the case, was Robert Trenton. He fanned the bristles with his thumb, searching for bits of paint. No flecks had landed on his white smock or creased khakis.

"That's a nice painting," admitted William, startling the man, who two-stepped sideways to hide his work.

"I didn't know you were standing there." Trenton collapsed the easel so it couldn't be seen. "I don't like people seeing my ..."

"Why? If I painted that well, I'd show it to people ... at least to my family."

The man let out a small, bitter laugh. "Especially not." He hurried away, case in hand.

If it hadn't been for the grinning devil's face adorning the ceramic clock, William would have walked right by the Now & Then Antiques shop. The clock chimed nine o'clock. A man strode up to the front door and unlocked it. He wore an old-style tuxedo with tails and a stovepipe hat like Abraham Lincoln's. He closed the door and flipped a sign: *Harry Pierce, Antiquarian, at your service.*

As William hurried past he thought this purple-painted antique shop would have looked strange in Toronto. Here on the hilly road sloping up from the harbour it looked just right among the other vividly painted houses.

A little restaurant opened to the street. William could smell bacon frying. His hand shot to his stomach. He had finished his mom's lunch on the first day. Last night he had found an apple forgotten on the bus. He had polished it on his jacket and consumed it very slowly with sips from his water bottle. He had even eaten the bruised parts and the core.

William spotted a Maritime Tel and Tel pay phone inside the diner. He went in and dialled his mother's number in Toronto. He would have used his dad's old cellphone but the battery was dead and he'd forgotten the charger.

The diner's lone customer, an RCMP police officer, held out his cup for more coffee. "Some kids tried to steal the weathervane from Trenton's place last night."

Wasn't Trenton the name of the painter?

The cook was a large black man with a knee-length white apron. He poured with an elegant up-and-down motion like he was pumping the black, steaming liquid out of the carafe. "Too much time on their hands."

William dialled the long-distance number.

Clusters of ketchup, mustard, and apple cider vinegar bottles waited to garnish meals at all twelve tables.

The policeman poured sugar and a dollop of milk into his coffee. Then he snapped the lid on his reusable cup. "Well," started the policeman, "I've got to go out and see Old Man Taylor. He said he saw a schooner last night, without its running lights. Apparently had a red jib."

The reference to the red jib caught William's attention. An automated voice from the phone company told him the call would cost four dollars and eighty cents for three minutes. He deposited the coins. They clanged their way into the belly of the phone. It rang and rang and rang.

His mother's voicemail kicked in: "You've reached Ferne and William. Please leave a message and we'll get back to you." William was annoyed with his mom but still liked hearing her voice.

The beep prompt brought him back to the moment. Soon enough the jig would be up. She'd know he'd run away. He snapped the receiver back in its cradle. The connection had been made, so he didn't get his money back. Then he felt weak and dizzy from lack of food. He leaned against the phone. The cook's stare straightened him up.

He counted the change from his pocket and checked the menu above the grill. There was nothing he could afford.

The cook flipped ham from the grill into the officer's takeout container. He watched William sniff as breakfast was carried past him. The officer raised his cup goodbye.

William spied a half-eaten muffin on a plate. The customer had slipped a five-dollar bill under the cup. William scooped up the muffin and headed for the door.

"Hey," called out the cook.

William turned defiantly. What did it matter if he took the

muffin? It had been abandoned — it was just going to be thrown out, anyway. And he hadn't taken the money.

"You shouldn't eat off o' someone else's plate," the cook said in a friendly voice.

William blinked. He tried to keep his hand from shaking before replying in a tone he hoped was natural. "I thought it was, like, you know, just left there."

"Was. Could make you sick, though. So how 'bout some toast?" The man busied himself scraping his grill and wiping down a counter that did not look like it needed it.

"I've only got thirty-two cents," William mumbled. He could feel himself blush with embarrassment.

The cook washed his hands. He pulled out the tail end of a loaf of bread. "This is day ol' bread. Why don't I make you toast with this? Boss don't like day ol' kept 'round. Perfectly good, mind you."

Why would this man be generous to him? He'd just tried to walk out with a leftover muffin.

"On the house, okay?" The cook didn't wait for his answer. He slipped two pieces of whole wheat bread into the toaster with a practised stroke of the wrist.

William smiled in agreement. The cook gestured to a stool opposite the front counter.

William dropped his backpack in front of his legs. He rested his weary self on the stool. He delighted in spinning it left and right. There was nobody else in the small restaurant, customer or boss.

Dishes stacked above the deep sinks spoke of breakfast guests other than the police officer.

The cook reached under a counter. "Got a couple o' cracked eggs here for you."

The two eggs he scooped from the grey cardboard carton looked intact.

With a tap the yolks slid and sizzled to a stop beside the bacon. He flicked the shells into a green compost bin.

Saying thank you, William tucked into the steaming plate of eggs, bacon, and toast. The glass of orange juice just appeared, so William smiled and nodded his thanks.

"You're from away?"

William swallowed a mouthful of egg and nodded. "On my way to see my grandfather, Daniel McCoy, over at his sail shop."

The cook shot a look at the wall clock. "Likely still at the Legion hall."

William wanted to ask him how he knew. But if he started asking questions the cook might ask a few of his own. Meanwhile, the cook gave him a map of downtown Lunenburg printed on a paper placemat. He circled the Legion's location.

The cook hoisted his large frame onto the counter. He pulled a cigarette from his pocket and lit it. He turned the exhaust fan over the grill up a notch and blew the smoke up the vent. He kept his hand up there to hide the cigarette.

"Boss don't allow no smoking in here. But I don't see no boss here, do you?"

William slurped up some egg yolk and toast. He pointed to a no-smoking sign. "Government doesn't allow smoking in here either." William's eyes locked with the cook's. The cook arched an eyebrow. William realized he had challenged him. "But I don't see them in here either … do you?" he added hurriedly.

The man took a long, slow scan of the empty restaurant and shook his head.

William took a bite of his toast and peeked over his shoulder. He shook his head, to assure the cook they were of a same mind. William wiped his hands on the paper napkin.

He scooped up his backpack. "Thanks for the breakfast. It was really good. Almost as good as my mom's." William winced at the thought that he had insulted him.

A smile crept to the corners of the man's mouth, "Can't do better than that."

"When I get some money, I'll come back and pay you."

The cook shook his head. "When you get settled, come back and have breakfast sometime."

William nodded. "Say thanks to your boss. What's his name?"

"Boss's name is Manny." His hand came out of the hutch vent without a cigarette.

"He sounds pretty cool," added William, shaking hands.

"He's okay," the big man replied.

On the sidewalk William took a breath of briny air and smiled at the sun. A man brushed by him and entered the diner. William heard him say "Morning, Manny" to the cook, who was looking out from behind the railing at William. William smiled and waved. Manny waved back.

Chapter Four

Dogs and the Devil

Banquette: a long bench in a sailboat's cockpit

The clip-clop of horse hooves drew William's attention to a tourist couple in a red-wheeled wagon that had room for four, maybe even six, passengers. The guide/driver sat on a bench at the front. His dad had promised to take him for a ride last summer. Maybe his granddad or granny would take him this year. The horse was a big beige draught horse, bred for pulling loads more than for riding. William thought it was a Percheron, just slightly smaller than a Clydesdale. The broad hooves covered in hair stopped for the tour guide's talk.

"Lunenburg's designation as a United Nations World Heritage site means that all of the buildings in Old Lunenburg have to respect their original architecture. They can't be torn down and replaced with new buildings, nor can they be repaired just any old way."

That's why everything looked out of time, William thought. He glanced at Manny's map.

"Why are they painted such bright colours?" asked one of the passengers.

"See, many of these houses once belonged to sea captains who painted their houses with paint left over from their schooners. Since the schooners were all different colours, so were the houses. The town was named in honour of King George II, who was also Duke of Braunschweig-Lüneburg."

A click of the guide's tongue moved saddle soap and horse smells past William. He followed them to Duke and Cumberland streets. The guide pointed out St. John's Anglican Church, rebuilt, he said, after the accidental fire in 2001. Close by was the old fire hall. Across the way was a two-storey building in blue and white with gold trim bearing a sign, *Royal Canadian Legion, Branch 23.*

A girl in a checkered shirt, a bit taller than William, slid out of the building. Blond head down and stiff-legged, she jangled car keys against her jeans. A man with salt-and-pepper hair burst out behind her. He whipped out a cigar and lit it with the movements of a much younger man. He puffed the cigar to life with a head back tilt before sending the smoking match arcing to the grass on his left. A southpaw is what his dad would have called this lefty.

"Excuse me. I'm looking for my grandfather, Daniel McCoy."

The girl's puzzled "oh" broadened into a smile. "Will! Oh, my God, I didn't recognize you. You've changed since last year. You've, um, you've grown." William tucked in his wrinkled shirt and smoothed back his greasy hair. This girl with the white-toothed smile looked faintly familiar.

"I'm Harley, Emmett's granddaughter, remember? We're cousins," she added, walking through the fog of smoke wafting their way. Harley fanned it as she reached for the man's shoulder.

"Grandpa, guess who's here from Toronto?"

"What's that? Louder and funnier, please," he said, cupping a hand to his ear. Then he broke into a smile. "William!" he said, spreading his arms to give him a hug.

"You probably don't remember me," Emmett said as William retreated a step.

"This is your great-uncle Emmett McCann, my grandfather," added Harley, plucking Emmett's cigar from his outstretched hand.

"I'm your grandfather's cousin. Just call me Emmett. Look how tall he's grown, Harley. So glad you came. Where's Ferne? And why didn't you call? We'd have picked you up from the airport." He snatched his cigar back and tucked it away from Harley.

"Uh, actually, I took the bus. Alone."

"Ferne let — your mother let you come all the way here alone? Without calling?"

"Uh, well, yeah, sort of."

"Sort of? It's either yes or no, William."

"Well, actually, I haven't talked to my mom yet."

"In plain English, William, does your mother even know you're here? Please, cut the crap. I hate it when people pour bilge water down my back and tell me it's raining."

Although his tone was even, Harley chimed, "Grandpa, you're being hard."

Emmett blew a puff of cigar smoke out the side of his mouth. "Well?"

"Well, uh … I left Mom a note. Told her I was camping. I called her when I arrived but I only got the answering … Sorry. I just wanted to see Granddad. I didn't …"

"A sensitive, caring boy would make sure his mom knew where he was, hmmm?"

Harley balled her fists on her hips and leaned forward with a reproachful stare.

"I'm not being hard," protested Emmett. "It just, well, it just sounds that way."

"It sounds hard? Heya, that's what I said."

"Then we agree."

"One of these days, Grandpa, I'm going to —"

"Whatever it is, put it on the calendar. I'll arrange to be out of town."

Emmett secured his cigar on a windowsill and led them inside.

She reached with the tips of her index finger and thumb like she would to pick up a slimy bug.

Emmett's voice boomed, "Dogs and the devil take you if you throw out that cigar."

"Why do you insist on smoking those horrible things, Grandpa?"

"It keeps the mosquitoes away." Emmett reappeared and snatched back his cigar.

"There are no mosquitoes."

"Obviously works," puffed Emmett with an impish grin.

"Will, you go ahead. We'll be in shortly," Harley directed. "Where to?"

Emmett flicked a finger to the lower floor. "Daniel's there with Reverend Strawbridge discussing tomorrow's memorial," he answered. Smoke wisped through his teeth like steam from a manhole cover in January. "Isn't that why you're here?"

He nodded. "Is Granny here, too?"

Harley and Emmett exchanged an awkward look. She answered. "Ah, well, she's in Halifax right now. Back tomorrow, of course. She's coming with my parents."

"What's she doing in Halifax?"

"She's, well, she's taking care of some business. Business stuff."

Chapter Five

Between a Rock and a Ferne

Sail loft: a loft or rooms where sails are cut and sewn together

Inside William was drawn to a black sign. The magnetic letters announced tomorrow's "Private function for the friends of Jack McCoy — downstairs." Now he remembered the place. Neighbours and friends had gathered here last year after his father's death.

A tall man with a clerical collar and a woman, probably Reverend Strawbridge and his wife, glided up the stairs like two people who didn't want to be heard leaving.

William stopped on the landing. He peeked into a room. It had high windows and panelled wood. The sunlight bathed his father's smiling photo on an easel. The same one had hung in his father's sail loft in Toronto.

Standing beside the easel was a stocky man with dishevelled grey hair. His grandfather's head tilted to the sunbeam as if resting his cheek on it for warmth. Sorrow etched Daniel McCoy's face. His small, confident smile had morphed into flat sadness. The year-long storm had battered him, too. The hunched shoulders didn't belong to the man William had left home to find. This wasn't the Rock who would shelter man or beast from gale, gun, or grief.

William had another look inside. Behind the photo a table offered beer and rum for tomorrow's visitors who wished to fill their hands with something to do during this awkward visit. There was also a pot of coffee.

His mind was crowding with faces that had been there last year, leaning in to him, hands tapping his shoulder, patting his hair in an assumed familiarity. He heard a chorus of "Sorry for your troubles … Sorry for … Sorry … Your troubles … Your troubles. Troubles."

Now he couldn't hear anything but ringing. Panic spun him around and propelled him towards the front entrance. He stopped a few feet from the door. He hadn't come all the way to the east coast to leave empty-handed. He forced himself to turn back. The ground-floor door creaked open to a flood of sunlight and a dying conversation between Emmett and Harley. They turned towards him.

William whispered, "Granddad looks so old. This is the same room, isn't it?"

Emmett bobbed his head. "The same room they used for your father's wake? Yes." He walked William over to his grandfather, who seemed unaware somebody was there.

"Daniel, look who's come all the way just to be with you." Daniel seemed focussed on Jack's photo and a different time. He didn't respond as Emmett straightened his jacket collar and smoothed back a wisp of hair.

The awkward silence drew him back to the present. Daniel peered at William. "Jack? Is that you, Jack?" Everyone said William was the spitting image of his dad when he was a boy.

His granddad's voice hadn't the deep presence he remembered. It sounded tired and thin from lack of practice.

"Uh, no, Granddad. I'm his son, your grandson, William. I just arrived on the bus from Toronto."

Daniel's mouth moved but no sound came out. He tried to process this bit of information. Then he looked to the table covered in refreshments. "Toronto? Oh, yes, of course. Would you like a glass of rum after your long trip?"

"Uh, well, I don't drink rum, Granddad. I'm just thirteen."

"Really? Happy Birthday to you, lad. A glass of beer, then?" asked Daniel.

William tried to keep a straight face. "Actually, I don't drink beer either, Granddad."

"Perfectly sensible of you. Alcohol has been the downfall of many a good man. How do you take your coffee?"

"Coffee? Well, uh, I guess I'll take it like you do, Granddad," said William about his first-ever coffee. Emmett and Harley smiled at him encouragingly.

Emmett waved William over. "Let's call your mother, shall we?"

"Now?" he cringed.

Emmett sat in an alcove by the door using the visitor phone. William stood staring at the tiles. He wondered who had dropped the toothpick sticking out from under the chair.

He'd been so sure that his only living grandparents were his salvation and would invite him to stay. He never anticipated this. The phone rang in their Cabbagetown house in the heart of Toronto. Emmett activated the speakerphone. William wouldn't miss a moment of his mother's reaction.

"Hello?"

"Ferne?"

"Yes."

"It's Emmett. Emmett McCann."

"Emmett? Emmett, my goodness. How are you?"

The speakerphone made his mother sound like she was trapped

at the bottom of a hole. William pictured her. She would be wearing jeans and a T-shirt. She'd be at the kitchen table in front of her laptop. She'd lick her finger and flip through newspapers and magazines to the advertising section. Her lower lip would be black with ink.

The ads she'd placed to promote the soon-to-open boat shows would have been circled with a red pen. Promoting boat shows across the country was her job. That's how they paid the bills now that they'd closed down his father's sailmaking business.

William's dad had said what his mother lacked in size she made up for with character and a great smile. He had been angry at his father for slowing her once-quick smile. Now here he was about to do the same.

"I'm calling about the pleasure of having William with us."

Silence. William held his breath.

"We're glad he's here with us, Ferne," Emmett continued.

"He's what?" Ferne asked.

"Ferne —"

"But, he's, he's camping …"

"Don't worry, Ferne. The boy's fine. He's safe. He's with us for the memorial."

"How did he get all the way — the memorial?"

"Oh Lord … Daniel didn't call." It was more a statement than a question.

"He hasn't spoken to me since Jack's funeral. Mary sent us an invitation but I thought it best … Will's been angry with me for … What about getting him home?"

Emmett glanced at William. "Look, Ferne, why doesn't the lad stay with us for a bit? Do us all good to have him here. School's almost over, isn't it?"

"He finished his exams, so there are only a few more days, class outings mostly."

William dreaded explaining himself to his mother.

"That settles it, then. Don't worry. Here he is."

"Wait, Emmett. He, uh, since the accident William has been prone to nightmares."

"Yes, well, there's some of that going around." He handed William the phone.

"Hello," he said in a defiant tone. He expected her to say she was supremely upset with him, with ice-cold composure to mask the fire beneath it.

"William?" she said, and he was sure he heard her crying.

"Mom?"

"Why did you leave me?" Her voice broke.

Harley escorted Daniel through the lobby and Emmett saved him. "Tell your mother you'll call her later. Mustn't keep your granddad waiting."

"Granddad's leaving, so I have to go now." Silence. "I'll call later. Bye."

Emmett muttered, "Dogs and the devil."

Chapter Six

The Derelict House

Schooner: a sailing vessel with at least two masts, with the foremast being smaller

They stopped at the sail shop. Harley said she only needed a few minutes to pack the meal she'd prepared for his grandfather. William pulled out the dog-eared card. He compared the drawing to the real front window. The bronze sailing trophy in the drawing wasn't in the window now. His father's death had prevented his grandfather from racing last year. If you didn't race, you didn't win.

Decades of sun had bleached the floor of the trophy case. In the middle was a dark circle of the original honey-coloured varnish where the missing trophy had sat.

There was a photo of the trophy on a poster advertising "The Old Lunenburg Classic Boat Race. Register Now!"

From left to right photos in the display case marked the decades-long history of the famed trophy with the bronze schooner on top. The photos started in black and white. They gained colour as they moved to recent years.

The man holding the trophy was his grandfather. He could see where his father, Jack, had inherited his features. It was an aging process his father wouldn't experience.

In one of the photos, his father was in his late twenties. He stood beside his grandfather on the deck of the schooner *Mary*. Wasn't that the schooner losing the race in Trenton's painting?

William sprang from Emmett's SUV to help Harley with the food containers. She locked the door to the loft and nodded towards the harbour. "Anybody lucky enough to live by the ocean … is lucky enough." She patted the building like a pet she was saying goodbye to and sighed. Aware he was watching, she smiled and said, "C'mon, let's go."

From Emmett's meandering SUV the clouds' pink hues looked like reflections of a distant blaze they were heading towards. The breeze drew William's attention to the fishing boats riding at their moorings in the little bays. The wind dropped. The boats swayed to their own rhythm. Then it gusted. All the boats turned their bows to the wind, lining up in perfect order, as though the breeze was a conductor bringing his wind instruments to attention.

"Wow, there are a lot of those boats," he said.

"Good design, those Cape Islanders," replied Emmett. "Their high bow allows them to handle rough seas. Small pilot houses and a long open stern make them ideal for pulling in fish nets or lobster traps."

The hulls were often white, but the trim colour varied with the tastes of their owners: royal blue, grass green, pomegranate red, pitch black, and canary yellow, to name a few. Just as colourful as their houses, thought William.

"These replaced the fishing schooners," Emmett added. "Motors replaced sail because they were more reliable. They weren't as quiet, as attractive, or as graceful. But they won out because of sheer effectiveness." He shook his head. "The bigger trawlers are so effective they've pretty well emptied the oceans of fish. So efficient they've killed the industry … and the livelihood of small fishermen."

Everybody could have done with seeing a whale with a polka dot tail or pigs with wigs. Instead, awkward silence crowded the car like slippery seaweed on the shore at low tide. Nobody wanted to venture there.

Down a peninsula they passed a new house with a grand metal gate. He was startled to see the painter's name, Trenton, above the archway. A whole bunch of trees had been felled to give the house a too-large clearing at the front. Past the windowed garage, the property ran to rocks, a dock, and ocean.

William saw the garage's sailboat-shaped weathervane.

"Some kids snuck in there and tried to steal the weathervane. The guard chased them away," Harley explained. That's what the policeman had said at Manny's.

"Oh," exclaimed William. His granddad followed the direction he pointed in. In a little tower off to the side of the second floor, the circular windows gave a clear view of the sailing trophy. The one that had so long lived in the display window of D & E Sailmakers was now here. His granddad seemed puzzled to see it there. The water visible through the window behind the trophy made it look like it had been washed up there after a storm.

The SUV veered between two waist-high rocks that squatted like sumo wrestlers, daring anyone to approach. The painted white stripes warned vehicles against an aggressive turn at night. The long driveway snaked up to an isolated, two-storey clapboard house on a peninsula overlooking the Atlantic.

"Careful with the water here, William," warned Emmett. "It's perfectly good. But it can play tricks on city folk not used to its high mineral content." He patted his stomach.

About five hundred metres offshore lay a pine tree-dotted island that buffered the shore and his grandfather's house from the Atlantic's fury. To the right of the island was a bay marked by a sandbar.

A boat could get to the ocean from his grandfather's place one of three ways: to the left, taking the long way around the island; past the rocks that extended into the ocean; or through what the locals called the Funnel, the passage between the island and the sandbar. It widened into a bowl-like middle. Easier for a boat to go through with a motor than a sail, like the Cape Islander that was chugging through it now and turning to open water.

His grandfather got out of the van and tottered towards the house, outstretched arms flicking for balance. He roamed as though in search of something he'd lost, then moored his sorrow on the veranda's rocking chair.

Harley turned to William. "It looks pretty derelict, but I love it here." She handed him some of the dinner containers to carry inside.

William took in the peeling white paint on the house, the covered-over well, the oversized utility shed, and an old tractor with foot-long grass between its tires. Tangled bushes sloped to an old boathouse by the ocean. He remembered more tidiness when they had buzzed in and out of here for the funeral.

The garden was populated by a tribe of driftwood carvings. The layered pieces resembled storks, pelicans, and albatross. He thought they would have flown to a happier place in a wing beat.

He delivered the dinner containers to the kitchen. Harley put some in the fridge. The rest she left on the counter before joining the others outside. He two-handed a dictionary from a row of books and looked up *derelict*. It meant "neglected." His granddad's place wasn't in ruins. It certainly was neglected, though.

His father's name was pencilled on a frayed game of Scrabble sitting beside the dictionary. Scrabble wasn't Brad's game. William even caught him cheating once when the board was bumped. One of Brad's blank tiles was in fact an "e" he had turned over.

When he hefted the dictionary back on the shelf, a dried purple flower fell from between the pages. He flashed on a memory of those flowers at the back of the house.

William slipped outside by the back door. He held the screen door so it wouldn't clatter. When he was a little boy his grandmother had helped him wield the too-heavy watering can. He remembered the sound of children's laughter and adults laughing too.

When he rounded the corner he saw that the old tree swing lay broken on the ground. The rhododendron bush reached above the kitchen window. It offered sick shoots, green leaching to brown.

Would there ever be more vanilla ice cream melting through the crispy brown sugar of Granny's hot apple crisp? Her sun hat and flowery gardening gloves lay on the seat of a weathered chair tucked under the long overhang. He reached out to touch the long silk scarf that ringed the hatband. It tore from rot and neglect.

Nothing was the way it used to be.

Chapter Seven

Dead Man Sailing

Ahoy: a sailor's call to attract attention, akin to hello

William wiped his tears and runny nose with his sleeve. He must be tired, that's all. That's what his mother always said whenever she cried over his father. Tears never helped achieve anything.

He washed and dried his face at the kitchen sink. His grandmother must be busy with something really important to let her garden dry up like this. According to Harley, she'd be back for tomorrow's memorial.

A flick of his index finger popped the eyehooks on either side of the window screen. Like his grandmother had shown him, he made sure the water wasn't too cold. He pulled the shower head out of the sink and gave the bush a desperately needed drink.

On the veranda, William noticed an old-style school bell secured to the wall. The inscription refused to fade in the oxidized brass: *To Mary McCoy in honour of her retirement, from three decades of students and faculty of the Academy. We have all learned from her humanity and dedication to teaching.* Okay, but where was she?

In the front yard he saw the last rays of the sun playing off the water. This wasn't the homecoming William had counted on. One smiling grandparent wasn't here. The other wasn't saying much of anything, let alone smiling.

Harley rang the brass bell to gather everyone to dinner at the picnic table. He half enjoyed the meatloaf, onions, green beans, rice, and coleslaw that Harley had prepared. It wasn't the joyous meal he'd dreamed of on the bus. Maybe sneaking away to Lunenburg hadn't been such a great idea. Now he felt guilty about wondering whether his grandmother's absence was going to complicate his dream of being allowed to stay with them. He might have to go back and deal with Brad and his mother.

Everyone was gone. His grandfather had retired for the night. William lay on the bed in his father's old bedroom with *Treasure Island* but was too distracted to read.

He studied the two sets of horizontal pencil markings on the door jamb. One set marked his father's annual height until his eighteenth birthday. The other marked his own height until age eight. He'd been a couple of inches taller than his father at the same age. They hadn't visited after William's eighth birthday. His dad had been too busy renovating their house and trying to make a living in Toronto.

There were photos on the wall of his father racing sailboats and as a student, working in D & E Sailmakers like Harley did now. The shelf was lined with small trophies, mostly for sailing. Hanging in the cupboard was his father's Dalhousie University rowing team jacket. The black and gold colours still looked sharp despite dust on the shoulders. On a shelf by the bed he spied a hand-carved model of a dinghy. It was signed "Jack McCoy" and wore the number "16" on its sails.

He listened to the ticking of the grandfather clock downstairs mingling with the steady rhythm of whooshing waves through the two open seaside windows. It almost lulled him to sleep. He forced his eyes wide open. The sooner he talked to his granddad about his problems, the sooner he could tell his mother of his plans to stay here, away from Brad and in a house that wasn't going to be sold out from under him. He went downstairs. He'd promised to call his mom.

From the kitchen stool he listened as his home number rang, three times, four times. It was an hour earlier in Toronto. He could picture her in their kitchen clipping discount coupons to hang on the pin board next to the calendar. She had taken down the honeymoon photo of her and his dad in Paris. She might stare at the photo of the two them smiling at him as a baby, sleeping in the belly of a sail with "16" stitched on it.

The same photo hung right beside him now on a cupboard in this kitchen.

"Ferne McCoy's residence," a man answered.

He felt himself flush with anger. Yes, it was Ferne's home. Our home. So what was Brad doing answering the phone at this hour? At any hour? He hung up.

He crept back upstairs and tiptoed down the hallway and knocked on his grandfather's door. No answer. He knocked again — nothing. "Granddad, I have a favour to ask you." He put his ear to the door and listened. A frightened animal's wailing clawed through the door. He'd never heard his father or his grandfather cry before. His granddad was just like his mother. They cried when you asked questions.

He retreated back to his father's old room.

"You and your stupid sailboats!" moaned William, grabbing the model boat. He reached back to fling it sidearm through the open window. He was stopped cold, his gaze drawn to the moonlit ocean.

A red jib pulled an unmanned schooner along the shore. A

familiar shadowy figure appeared in the cockpit. He waved to William.

The curtains on the window where he stood were blowing back. Those on the room's other window, ten feet away, were absolutely still. What kind of wind only blew at one window?

William looked from the far curtains to the window in front of him. The schooner had disappeared. The wind died altogether. He placed the model back where it belonged and shot a look at the glass of well water by his bed. Was this the kind of trick Emmett had warned him about?

Rattled by images of boats, now here, now gone, he went downstairs to phone his mother again. This time she answered.

"I almost died when Emmett said you were in Lunenburg." There was hurt in her voice. A small piece of him would have preferred the "supremely annoyed" treatment. "Can't believe you went all the way there for … A memorial is just postponing the inevitable. Dragging it out."

"We can't forget about Dad overnight, Mom. We can't wash it all away after just a year."

"Depends on the year, Will." She blew her nose. "Why didn't you tell me you were —"

"Why didn't you tell me you had a new boyfriend?"

"Brad's not my boyfriend. Just somebody from work who's … become a friend. Somebody who wants to see me, and us, happy."

"It's not working. He should just back off. Or are you going to marry him?"

"It's a little early to be talking marriage." She laughed.

"It's a little early to be seeing somebody. A fake, a guy who, who's … nothing like Dad."

She sighed. "Oh, Willy-boy, he's just a nice guy who's … trying to be there for me."

William left a long pause to voice his disbelief and disapproval.

"He was just here helping me sort through your father's things."

"He shouldn't be touching any of Dad's things," he snapped.

"I tried —"

"He shouldn't be there at all!" he thundered.

There was another long pause.

"You'll get to know your cousin Harley, spend time with her. That's good."

Silence.

"Do you want me to send you some money, maybe your allowance?"

"I'm okay on my own," he lied.

"Oh Willy-boy, these are tough times, aren't they?" she asked, stating the obvious. "I miss you already." She left him room to tell her he missed her. He didn't.

"Okay, well, goodbye then," she offered.

Silence.

"And good night." She said it like she always did, like he was in the same room, not half a country away. "I love you, Willy-boy."

He laid the phone back in its cradle, hoping she would appreciate that he'd put it back gently. He ran his index and middle fingers along the receiver, reaching out to her in a way his anger wouldn't allow him to voice.

Too wired to sleep, he walked into the living room and looked for something to watch on the DVD player. On the shelf he found a few DVDs he'd seen. There was one marked "The Rescue of Daddy's Girl." He had seen his father's copy a long time ago.

He turned on the television and the DVD player. He slipped the DVD in and pressed play.

The original footage had been film his father had copied for family members. William played the sound low so as not to disturb his grandfather.

It was grainy TV news footage shot in a storm. The wind tore at the reporter's raincoat as he brought his microphone closer. "The South Shore was rocked by an early August storm today. It was no place for fish or fowl, who all took refuge where they could. The Coast Guard had every man and boat out for rescue operations up and down the coast, so there was nobody to answer the mayday call put out by the three-man crew of the fishing boat *Daddy's Girl* when she took on water and began to founder. The Coast Guard was too far off and nobody would face the wrath of the Atlantic — except skipper Daniel McCoy and his three-man crew in a daring rescue we were able to capture on film."

Now the cameraman was positioned up on a cliff. Between the blasts of rain one glimpsed a schooner. She had bare poles except for her storm jib wrestling for control from wind and battering waves. The cameraman tried to zoom in. He settled for a wide shot. The schooner ran up beside the sinking boat. Two fishers leapt from the roof of her pilothouse onto the schooner's open deck where McCoy's crew pulled them in.

The reporter narrated over images of the rescue. "It seemed impossible that the schooner could run so close without smashing her hull against the partially submerged boat, but she did. The last man still aboard the sinking craft had broken his leg. He wasn't able to leap. So McCoy's cousin, Emmett McCann, lashed himself to the far end of the main's boom. The skipper sailed her with his cousin hanging from that boom. He timed the swell of tide and wind to dip him close enough to grab the injured man without smashing the rescuer on the Cape Islander's roof."

The camera captured rescuer and victim clinging to each other at the end of the boom. Refusing to give up its prey, the ocean swung at them with a pounding wave. "On deck, their backs bent, the two crews pulled the line hand over hand till they freed the two men from the staggering weight of water. With the wounded fisher snatched from the cold Atlantic, McCoy brought his crew, the rescued party, and his boat safely back to port."

The storm had abated when the image cut to the Lunenburg dock. An ambulance crew rolled the wounded man on a gurney. Colour had returned to the screen but the fisherman's face was ashen with pain when he spoke. "We was done for. Sunk. When dis ghost boat appeared to pluck us from certain death. The man was a rock. A rock."

The image jumped to a man, beaming at being alive with his crew mates, shaking the water from his hair. The reporter slid opposite him on the dock. It was Emmett with less grey hair but the same lean build.

"Mr. McCann, weren't you frightened out on that boom?" He snapped the microphone over the gunwale for Emmett's reply.

Emmett flashed his impish grin. "Not nearly as frightened as I would have been behind the wheel. You see the way Daniel surfed down the side of that wave then took her to starboard?" His hands reenacted the rescue. "He rode the motor so we could crest just as the roof and that fisher rose to us. Dogs and the devil take him, that man's got more nerve than a barge horse." The crew's nervous laughter drowned out any thought they might well not have come back.

The image jumped to William's father, Jack, at around his age, holding Daniel's dripping life jacket and walking beside him. His face was turned up to him in awe. Daniel waved off the journalists' questions with an answer as simple as his smile. "Excuse us. The lad and I need a cup of tea."

"Well, that was just, just amazing," sputtered the journalist.

Young Jack tilted his head up to the microphone. "My dad's like that."

The reporter commented, "There goes Daniel McCoy, a two-legged piece of granite holding his son's hand, undeterred by the riptide of questions trying to pull them back to the cameras." The reporter closed with a subdued, "Must be nice to have a hero for a dad."

William turned off the TV and DVD player. He felt better when he heard the reporter speak of his grandfather as the "hero" he was going to ask for help.

His grandmother was coming back for the memorial. Surely she'd understand his need to get away from Brad and find some place to be a regular.

Chapter Eight

Idle Hands

Jib: a small rectangular foresail

William trudged ahead of Harley, looking to see if his granny had arrived. She hadn't. He was behind Emmett, who was behind Daniel, when they walked into the cemetery for the memorial. He spotted the antique dealer's Abe Lincoln hat peeking above faces he didn't know. Manny was there. He clasped his hands in front of him. Positioned away to his left was the painter, Robert Trenton.

Off to a side, head bowed, stood a vested piper, tartan kilt, sporran, a dirk in his knee socks and his pipes by his side — full Highland sadness. There had been a piper at the funeral, too. Come to think of it, there had been a large group of men his father's age, all wearing rowing team jackets. If they were here, they weren't wearing those jackets today.

He remembered a painting in his father's sail loft. It showed a piper playing at the dock as a sailboat spirited Scottish immigrants from their homeland to what they hoped would be a better future. The sorrow he remembered from that canvas was painted on faces here in the graveyard.

There was a folding table beside his father's gravestone.

Whatever was on the table was covered by a cloth that looked like a piece of sail material.

He was going to ask Harley about it when she leaned in and whispered, "The Academy." She pointed beyond the cemetery to the sprawling red and white schoolhouse. It had served generations of Lunenburg children. He remembered that the inscription on the brass bell had told him his grandmother had taught there. His father had attended. He would have attended if they hadn't moved to Toronto.

Four rectangular turrets reached above the roofline. That painted a spooky fairy-tale image. Who but the brothers Grimm would put a school next to a graveyard with no fence? Schoolchildren could just walk through any old time. Maybe fishermen and sailors didn't put barriers up between life and death. Maybe that's why his father had found it so easy to make his way here.

Harley nudged William. She pointed her chin to a car pulling up. William's grandmother slid out of the passenger seat. She wore the same colourful dress she had worn in the birthday card photo. Her smile wasn't so much flashed as hoisted. She took Harley's father's hand.

His grandmother went right over to Daniel. She gave him a kiss on the cheek. He raised a hand as though to make a point, then let it drop. He shuffled sideways to let her stand between himself and Emmett.

William stepped towards her and was rewarded with a broadening smile. She rocked him with an upper-body sway. These were not the robust arms of the woodcutter who saved Red Riding Hood or those of the Prince who saved Snow White. There was no apparent saviour from his grim fairy tale.

"I'm glad you're here." She gave him a squeeze. "How are you getting along with your grandfather?"

"Doesn't do much except sit in his rocking chair."

"He's earned his porch privileges. He'll get over it when this ..." She waved her hand by her side to dismiss the assembled grief. "I'll be back for good when I've finished up in Halifax."

He thought she'd beam at his daring, be proud of her grandson's cleverness in coming all the way here. What could be more important than being with him and his grandfather?

Daniel held a photo of Jack over his heart. Family and friends scrunched around them. It made him think of elephants leaning together to stop a wounded member of the herd from falling.

Reverend Strawbridge droned an excerpt from the Bible. He ambled through his father's life like a new driver backing up. Hesitation and uneasy starts bumped towards a conclusion everyone was dying for him to find. Irritated clouds sprinkled drops of holy water to hurry the service's conclusion.

Emmett stepped in. "It gives me great pleasure, as chairman of the Old Lunenburg Classic Boat Race, to unveil our trophy that has been renamed 'the Jack McCoy Trophy,' in tribute to Jack's dedication to showing young people how to sail." Emmett pulled the cloth away to reveal the sailing trophy. William leaned in along with a few others to read the new silver band that bore his father's name.

Emmett continued. "Oh, and we're fortunate to have William, his son, here to help us remember him. It's been a year since Jack McCoy's death. An unexpected death in somebody so young and, well, so full of life. He taught us all the importance of dreaming. He said you couldn't make a better world unless you could imagine it. That a child without a dream gave everybody nightmares." Here he faltered a moment, cleared his throat, and then continued. "If you listen carefully, you'll hear him teaching the angels to sail."

His comments had mourners wiping their eyes. Harley's father gave her a squeeze, a father's squeeze William would never feel again.

"Amen," said the Reverend Strawbridge. The piper blew a skirl that screeched until the airflow levelled. His fingers moved up and down the chanter. Reverend Strawbridge's "Amazing Grace" proved that his strength was song.

Harley whispered, "We'll be heading over to the Legion before driving back up to Daniel's. You don't know these people so it's cool if you want to take your time getting back. Oh, and Mom and Dad brought you some of my clothes that should fit you. Don't worry; they're guy things that are just too small for me now."

William tried to smile. "Oh, ah, thanks. Thank your parents for me." Hand-me-downs from a girl — really? The mourners shuffled away murmuring, "Sorry for your troubles."

Daniel squatted to lay the photo on the mounded earth that looked like it was pushing back. In time, William thought, the mound would settle like all the other graves, resistance fading. Fading like memories of his father's hands that no longer steadied him.

Emmett crouched beside his cousin. "Not the natural order of things, Daniel. We bury our parents, our children bury us. Burying our children … just not right." He helped Daniel to his feet and they shuffled off.

William had complained to his mother about his father being buried too far away to visit. Yet standing here didn't feel any better. Emmett had hit the nail on the head; it just wasn't right.

He spotted Trenton, carrying the trophy, moving deeper into the graveyard to lean by a grave near the far end of the cemetery. He strode away and William headed up to where he'd stood and read the inscription on the headstone: *Thomas Trenton, beloved son and brother, now fishing with the Lord.* Thomas Trenton was not quite twenty years old when he had died some thirty years ago. Why had he died so young?

The next morning he hurried down to the kitchen, hoping his granddad would be fixing breakfast. Harley had done it yesterday when she and Emmett came to get them for the memorial.

There was no answer when William called out. He opened the fridge to find a dried slice of blueberry pie, a carton of orange juice, and leftovers. William grabbed some juice and slammed the fridge door.

The grandfather clock *ticked, ticked, ticked*; time was slipping away. He didn't know if he was staying or heading home and admitting defeat. He slapped the frame, kicked the screen door open, and stormed out.

A patch of garden by the veranda housed the tree people. They were small bulbs of tree roots that had been pummelled ashore where his father had found them. Now turned on their stumps, they looked like grey folk with thick dreadlock roots chaffed blunt by the ocean. They had once sheltered amidst greenery. They seemed surprised at their shrivelled habitat. He knew how they felt.

His grandfather's minivan had a coating of dust on it as though someone was burying it but was in no hurry to finish the job. His father had called it the Funmobile because it was always going off somewhere to do something fun. It smelled of oil and grease in a good way. A way that would fix things. His father said the Funmobile was always crammed with sailing gear and laughing people. Not anymore. It lay there, tires soft like muscles that would no longer move. Its sides were marked by rust blisters that leaked its lifeblood.

It made him think of an animal that had been shot, not for the food or clothing it could provide but simply because somebody could shoot it, did shoot it, and hadn't bothered to bury the corpse.

The utility shed looked more like a small barn with brass portholes. Decades ago his father and grandfather had salvaged the portholes and the wood from a shipwreck on the beach below.

Stepping by the tractor he pulled open one of the big doors. He saw gardening equipment and fishing gear. A sail draped over a beam above a dinghy that looked just like the model that sat on his bedside table. The sail also had number "16" on it.

The sail reminded him of a dream he'd had a number of times since his father's death. It wasn't a nightmare, not as bad as reliving the truck crash. It was more of a bad dream.

In it he found himself on a big sailboat with his father. That alone was strange because his dad had been too busy to take him sailing even when he was trying out sails for a client. "Can't watch you and how the sails perform," was his explanation. William knew it was a dream because he wasn't afraid of water as he was since the crash.

In this dream his father was always in the cockpit. Somehow it wasn't a cockpit but a sewing pit. His father sewed, head down, never looking at him. William called him, but his father couldn't hear him above the wind and the *thunka, thunka, thunk* of the industrial needle.

William always started the dream at the bow of the sailboat. His view of the sewing pit was mostly obstructed by sails, lots of billowing sails. He'd try to move towards his father. He'd push and lean against them. The overpowering sails pushed him back. When he finally got to the cockpit, his father wasn't at the sewing machine anymore. He had somehow gotten past William to the bow. There he looked up at his workmanship, never at William. He was busy running his hands along the sails he'd just finished making.

His father had been so clever with his hands, yet William couldn't even fix the broken swing. Why hadn't he taught him how to use his hands? Why hadn't his father gone to the doctor and just taken a pill or something for his heart like the ads said on TV? Instead he had just worried about sails. William took a deep breath and continued his exploration of the big shed.

He lifted the corner of a large tarp. Instead of a piece of equipment he found his father's pickup. Rust and mud covered the McCoy Sails logo. He glimpsed the slashed seatbelt that hadn't saved his father's life anymore than he had. He jumped back from the tarp and snarled in anger, "What good are your stupid sails, now, huh, huh?"

He turned to the bulging sail hanging over the beam and slapped it. Then he punched it again and again, to no effect. He jerked the weed whacker from its hook, tore at the pull cord till the steel blades whirred. He slashed the sail till there was nothing left but ribbons waving in surrender.

Chapter Nine

The Secret Tunnel

Rigging knife: a sailor's knife used in managing lines

William's stomach knotted. He threw up in a bucket. After his stomach had settled down, he rinsed his mouth out three times, then leaned against the sink to catch his breath. He released the eyehooks and pushed out the screen and watered the rhododendron with the sink's spray hose.

William's chest heaved from the effort of digging the hole behind the shed. He had placed his father's logo face up before shovelling dirt on top of the sail.

The place was getting on his nerves with the quiet, the absence of life and activity. He looked around. What change might he tackle first? He had to do something. He couldn't face his dad's truck, so resurrecting the Funmobile seemed an obvious choice.

He found a long faded green hose. It snaked through the tall grass like an emaciated boa. He sprayed off the first layers of grime that was part salt powder, part dust. He filled a bucket with soapy water. With a soft brush he scrubbed away the most upsetting sight — the blood-coloured rust stains running down its flanks.

He dried the windows. He took a bicycle pump and inflated the tires. The proper tire pressure sticker was on the inside of the door. The tire gauge was in the glovebox just like it was in his dad's truck.

Then he blended a gas and oil mix and filled the weed whacker like he did with the one they had in Toronto. He changed the steel blades in favour of nylon strings. He pulled on ear protectors, safety goggles, and a well-worn pair of gloves. He cut the tall grass for more than an hour.

The sun stretched its gaze to where Daniel now rocked on the veranda. A post kept his face away from the sun's reach.

William pulled his ear protectors off and swatted flecks of wet grass stuck to his pant legs. He called out. "Granddad, yesterday Uncle Emmett called to say he was driving over this afternoon. I thought I'd go into town with him for some groceries."

His grandfather rocked in and out of the gloom. William noticed his shirt was inside out. On the next tilt he saw patches of greying stubble his razor had missed. A fly landed on his granddad's hand. Unable to get his attention, it zigzagged away.

William heard, then saw, Harley biking up the laneway. She led a spare bike with her left hand. He didn't want to ask his granddad in front of her, so he hurried his request. "I, uh, could do with some money, for groceries and, uh, while I'm on the subject of eating here, Granddad, I was wondering if we could talk about me staying here with you for …" The fly buzzed back to answer.

William smacked his hands against his pants, helicoptering more shreds of grass back to earth.

"You're just like Mom and Dad. Never there when you need them," he grumbled.

William ignored Harley's reproachful stare. He clumped his gear back to the shed.

"I don't think that's nice of you, William."

"Is it nice that Granddad sits there, just waiting to ... and everyone keeping stupid sails around. Even Uncle Emmett said motors were more efficient."

She started to argue but stopped, threw her arms out, and said, "I brought you a bike."

William raised a hand in meek thanks. He realized she might have interpreted it as waving her off. Either way, she pedalled back to Lunenburg.

Another hour of weed whacking patched his shirt with sweat. William trudged into the kitchen for a glass of water. He held it to the light for inspection. The last thing he wanted were more visions of sailboats. A mouse skittered across the floor and disappeared under a kitchen island. William nudged the plinth with the toe of his shoe. It fell back.

He peered beneath the island counter and saw a faint light bounce off a shiny surface. His fingers reached a steel ring set into the floorboards. With a few grunts, he pushed the counter across the pine floor. He froze.

William called out the window, "Hey, Granddad, do you know you have a trap door here in the kitchen? Granddad?" Only the wind coming off the sea chimed an answer.

He pulled on the ring. It wouldn't budge. He tried tapping and heard a hollow sound under the trap door. He clasped the ring with both hands and flexed his knees till they burnt. Like everything in Lunenburg, the rusty hinges wouldn't yield to him.

He slipped the tip of the fireplace poker under the ring. A piece of firewood gave the poker three feet of leverage. It bowed a little under his weight but nothing more. He bounced his weight on the poker. The trap door jerked open with a rusty screech.

He swung the door open. A set of dusty wooden stairs led to a black, cobweb-filled tunnel. Wind whistled up the stairs. Then he heard a moan. A moment later there was another. "Hello," he called down. "Anyone there?" He didn't want to go down the spooky stairs, but what if someone was in trouble? He couldn't wait for his granddad to react. That might be too late.

Unable to find a flashlight, he settled for a lit candle in a jar. He shoved matches into his jeans pocket and risked one foot at a time down into the tunnel.

Wind shrilled along a dark passage ahead. Then he heard the moans again, this time closer. He yelped as he tripped over an empty crate with *Dark Rum, 1923* written in fading paint. His father had told him the house had belonged to a Nova Scotian rum-runner before Daniel had bought it.

He came to a wooden wall with a curtained partition on the left. Rusty lengths of chain hung before him, held together by ancient padlocks. The sounds came from behind the tattered partition. He crouched, drew back a dusty edge of the curtain, and held out the jar with the candle.

There, inches from his nose, was a grinning devil's face. He screamed. His backward leap sent him crashing through chains and rotten boards.

William smacked his head with a *thunk*. He landed face down on cold sand. He coughed, blinked, and listened to the ocean's surf licking the shore. He rolled over and looked up. The wooden hull of a boat in its cradle towered over him. He felt the back of his skull where it had hit the keel. The skin over the bump hadn't split. He would keep going.

Relieved by the sight of sunlight streaking in through cracks in the boathouse, William pushed on the doors. The rusty chain and padlock yielded only a couple of inches. He relit his candle. Then he crawled back through the splintered wood into the tunnel to investigate what had startled him. The devil's face — goatee, horns, and all — was painted on a ceramic pitcher. Beside it sat a matching bowl, decorated with an identical image. They were perched on a shelf in a small space. Beside it someone had jammed four chairs and a table with a dusty deck of cards.

He clambered through the splintered wood and rusty chains into the boathouse. The name on the boat's transom was *Fathom*. The hairs on his neck stood up. It was the same name as the boat in his dream. How could that be?

William climbed the wooden ladder to its spotless cockpit. He stared through the high window to the top of Daniel's house, a hundred yards away.

His eye went to a flash of light reflected in the cockpit. It was his dad's rigging knife. The words *William McCoy* in gold inlay in the handle left no doubt. He picked it up. How did it get here? How cool. Someone had found it at the wreck site, no doubt. Why leave it here? he wondered. He examined the four-inch blade and marlinspike, the long, tapered piece of steel flipped out of either end of the handle. There was no indication of rust. This was too weird. He pocketed the knife. There had to be a way back to sunlight without using the tunnel.

He grabbed the bowl and pitcher with the devil's face. The big doors were locked. The door on the side was held shut only by a small piece of wood that swivelled up and down into a catch. Strange, he thought, the latch was thick with dust but the cockpit was clean as a whistle. Maybe there was just more wind up there.

He pulled the door open and closed it, then shook it so the piece of wood fell back into the locking mechanism. He slipped the knife blade in the gap between the door and the frame and was able to lift the piece of wood out of the catch. He had figured out how to get in and out of the boathouse without using the tunnel. He picked up the bowl and pitcher and smiled at the devil.

Back at his grandfather's house, he washed and dried the bowl and pitcher. He placed them on a shelf just as Daniel trudged in, sloshing tea from his mug.

William took a cloth and wiped up the tea drips.

"Hey, Granddad, look what I found down there, behind the boatshed. The one with *Fathom* on its cradle. Why don't you sail *Fathom*?"

"My father, the Real McCoy, gave it to me. Probably to make up for the fact he only discovered he had a son in Lunenburg when I was a lad."

"That was nice of him. So why don't you sail *Fathom*?"

"I went to Halifax to meet him. But he'd already left Halifax. McCoy had bought that schooner and had done a detour by way of Saint-Pierre. By the time I came home, I found out he had murdered a man." William wasn't sure he'd heard correctly. Had his grandfather just told him the Real McCoy had murdered someone?

"Obviously I wouldn't have anything to do with a murderer. So McCoy left me a note."

"What kind of note?"

His granddad's face hardened. "We don't talk about that note in this house. Nobody in this house has anything to do with that boat. It's got a blood curse on it. I would have sold it except for McCoy's legal stipulation. *Fathom* has to stay in the family and not be sold outside the family." With that Daniel plunked his cup on the counter. He shuffled past him.

William wanted to ask about the murder. Who had died? Why? Was McCoy charged and found guilty? But he knew what happened when he asked his grandfather and his mother questions. Besides, Uncle Emmett was just driving up.

Emmett and Harley brought him and his bicycle into town. After her criticism he didn't feel like sharing his discovery of the tunnel or asking her about the murder. She sat in the front and stared straight ahead.

As they approached the Fisheries Museum, William spotted

a sign: *Help Wanted — Apply Within.* A job would make up for his missing allowance. He was afraid to ask his grandfather for pocket money. And after their blowup he sure couldn't ask Harley. "I think I'll stop off here at the museum, Uncle Emmett." He caught Emmett's stare in the rear-view and added, "Please."

"Good idea. There's a section on rum-runners — including your great-grandfather, the Real McCoy." Emmett pulled his vehicle over and added, "By the way, have you given any thought to entering this year's race with your grandfather? It's a McCoy tradition. Daniel used to love racing with Jack."

William didn't want to admit his fear of water since the accident. "Granddad doesn't look to be in any shape to handle a boat."

"Your grandfather will bounce back. Daniel was always what you might call the strong, silent type. Losing Jack's left him more silent than strong — a terrible blow."

"I know all about that," William blurted, impatient to inquire about the job.

Harley corkscrewed around. "Chill out, will you? You're angry at your dad for dying — fine. But stop taking it out on your granddad and mine."

Emmett's hand shot up like a stop sign. "Enough! Both of you."

"Oh, come on, Grandpa. He's not the only one with problems right now, right? We've got enough to worry about with Daniel's home, not to mention the loft —"

"Then let's not mention it," he pressed. "These are our problems, not William's."

"If he's part of this family —" Emmett's raised hand stopped Harley.

What was that all about? What was wrong with the sail loft? What was wrong with his granddad's house? With a shrug and a mumbled "thanks" to Emmett he unloaded his bicycle.

Emmett called out the window. "I'll drop some food off for you and Daniel a little later. Here's some money for your admission to the museum. Bye for now."

Inside, William was told that someone in human resources would be with him shortly. So he waited at the rum-runners exhibit. He stared at a photo. His great-grandfather, the Real McCoy, stood on a dock, wearing an old-style rain slicker and a fedora. It was identical to the one he'd seen on the schooner with the red jib. Maybe it wasn't the water. Weird stuff was happening in Lunenburg.

The plaque beneath the photograph read, "William (Bill) McCoy was one of the most successful rum-runners. He didn't water down his liquor. When patrons drank good liquor during Prohibition they said it was the *Real McCoy*." William peered more closely at the photograph. Could this man be a murderer?

"Hi, I'm Andrew Knickle, the museum —" The voice, blurted without warning, made William jump and bring his hand up defensively.

"You all right? You look as though you've seen a ghost," said Andrew Knickle. William stood up from his crouch. Mr. Knickle wore a tweed jacket with a paisley bow tie whose yellow flecks matched his shirt. "Are you here to see about the job?"

William nodded and forced a smile.

"Well, I'm afraid you're not old enough to know all that much about fishing history, but maybe come back in a few years and we'll see what we can do."

William's face turned red — with anger and embarrassment — but he thanked the man and quickly moved away, then burst through the doors of the museum and out onto Bluenose Drive.

As his dad would say, the way his fortunes were going it looked like he'd be lucky to catch a cold in Lunenburg. Was this town going to be his prison or his salvation?

Even the flat roads seemed uphill. He coasted his bike past the municipal ballpark. A handful of boys were practising baseball. And leading the practice was Manny. He held a bat straight up in front of his body.

As he tipped it to his left, the boys did the boxer's shuffle in that direction. Their bodies leaned forward, gloves at the ready, right foot extending out then followed by the left foot, shuffle, shuffle, shuffle. Then Manny tipped the bat over to the right like a slow-motion metronome. The boys shuffled never crossing their feet, never tripping either. William wished he had a coach to talk to.

He biked past the graveyard but kept his eyes on the road.

The sun was resting on a cloud by the time William reached the top of the driveway and leaned the bike against the house. His grandfather dozed in his veranda rocking chair. One side of his cardigan was crooked. It bulged where the button had skipped its hole. A cup sat on the armrest. A teabag floated at the top, cold, untouched.

"Hey, Granddad. Do you think we could talk now? I have something I need to tell you." Daniel answered with a gentle snore. Sleep had not removed the worry from his face.

He mumbled on the way in to the kitchen, "My day's been great so far. Thanks for asking."

He washed his hands in the kitchen sink. As he dried them his eyes fell on the rigging knife he'd laid on a shelf between the pitcher and bowl with the grinning devils.

"Granddad, I'm going back into town for a little bit, okay?" He pocketed the knife.

He popped the eyehooks to the screen on the window and swivelled it out as he'd done before. He tested the water temperature and watered his grandmother's rhododendron with the hose extension from the kitchen sink.

He called to his grandfather through the veranda. "I'm going to set fire to the Fisheries Museum and sink all the boats in the harbour, okay?"

He biked down the drive, rattling over the asphalt's web of splits seared by sun, salt, and snow. He gave wide berth to the white rock at the bottom, banked sharply onto the highway, then pedalled to Lunenburg. He passed fish shacks and the Cape Islanders back from their early morning work.

In the Now and Then Antique shop, Harry Pearce sipped sherry. The newspaper he read was dated 1894. He looked up so quickly the glasses clamped to his nose flew off. William caught them. These glasses had no temples. Pearce nodded his thanks as he clamped them back on his nose.

"They're called pince-nez," he explained. "Belonged to an early French settler. The prescription's new, of course. Harry Pearce at your service. What can I do for you?"

"I'm, uh, Will. Could you tell me what something might be worth?" He wasn't sure he wanted to sell his father's knife but he might just have to for money.

"You want an appraisal. Do you have the item with you, Master William?"

"Uh, yes, I do," William answered, glancing at the antiques. Some were suspended from the shop's rafters. There were a lot of brass fittings and wooden pieces from working boats long retired from the demands of the sea.

"Well? I take it we are not talking of an Edwardian chair or a Louis Quatorze desk?"

"I'm sorry, what?"

Pearce added, with a twinkle, "I gather it is a rather small object, unless of course you have deeper pockets than I thought?"

"Right, here it is. It's a ..."

Pearce's eyes lit up as he cradled the knife. "A whalebone-handled rigging knife." He flexed the blade before adding, "With gold inlay." He flexed the spike and noted, "The blade and marlin-spike are both French and have been well-maintained. The bone handle was added by a local skilled craftsman."

"How do you know all this?"

"If the right buyer were to come along it would be worth, let's say, two hundred dollars — minimum. At auction it might fetch five … maybe a thousand." William's mouth fell open. He continued, "If it did indeed belong to the Real McCoy." William shifted his weight under Pearce's gaze. "Is it yours? Yours to sell, I mean. Hate to have the police ask how I came into possession of a knife with the name William McCoy."

"The police? Well, I, I mean, William McCoy is my name." William retrieved the knife. "I'll think about selling it, thanks." The bell over the door clanged as he retreated.

Chapter Ten

Keelhaul

Spinnaker: a large sail used to sail downwind

A large, mounted salmon head flashing sharp teeth greeted visitors to his grandfather's sail loft. It overlooked the counter's cash machine and computer. An ashtray and a swivelling Scrabble game lay beside a model of a sloop whose spiky mast skewered a half-dozen invoices. The name on her transom read "Bill's."

The working area was divided in two. The first stretched from the office counter, where big sails were laid out for measuring and cutting. The three sewing pits reminded him of the Toronto sail loft where his dad had pulled sails through to sew them. He'd always finished a seam before looking up and smiling at him.

Rolls of sail material and plastic bins with things like stainless steel grommets were stowed beneath a thick-planked staircase. It led to an area used for smaller sails.

William followed the sounds of frying into the kitchen. These were Emmett's private quarters he shared with Harley when she worked here. Harley's foot tapped to the music.

She wheeled towards him with a raised cleaver and a diving mask on her face.

"Damn, you scared me," she said, turning down the radio. The mask gave her voice a funny, nasal quality. She yanked it off. "Onions — they make me cry. Sorry!" She laughed.

"Hello. Anybody home?" interrupted a voice. They quickly turned and saw a man entering the loft carrying a red canvas bag.

Harley turned off the stove, peeled off her apron, and skipped past William. "Good morning, Mr. Dingle."

"Morning, Harley."

Harley grabbed a paper he was holding. "You've filled out your racing form, I see. William, could you enter this data onto the computer, then hit print? Oh, Mr. Dingle, meet my cousin, Will McCoy."

"Hi, there, Will," he said, shaking William's hand. William said hello, and then watched as Mr. Dingle scooted through the loft and stared into the sewing pits as if he might catch someone hiding there.

William turned his attention to the task at hand. The computer was open at the website for the competition. He filled out the online form and noticed that Paul Dingle managed the local bank.

Emmett plodded down the stairs from the small work area. He slipped his scissors back into the sailmaker's holster on his hip. He sewed a piece of sail fabric on his way over. The needle was pushed through the fabric with the leather palm strapped to his right hand. William's father had owned a bunch of them. He knew the plastic over the meat of his thumb by the palm was dimpled like a golf ball. It secured the head of the needle. That way it wouldn't slip under pressure and pierce the user's hand.

Emmett scooped a half-smoked cigar from the ashtray and stuck it in the salmon's open mouth. "Makes him look like a gangster, doesn't it?" Emmett asked William. "We haven't had one robbery since Frank the Fish," he said, patting the fish head, "started chomping a stogy."

Harley made a face. "Oh, right, like we'd have a robbery here without it." She cut off Emmett's reply. "And don't tell me it obviously works."

He cracked a smile and swung a wink in William's direction.

"Granddad stuffs his old cigars in the fish's mouth," explained Harley. "Then I move them to the ashtray, and after a while they disintegrate and I'm allowed to throw them out."

"There you go, Mr. Dingle, your registration and copy of the rules — which I think you know, considering they haven't changed since I started writing them up — and deh, deh, deh, deh. How's the lending business these days, Mr. Dingle?" William caught the disapproving look Emmett shot her way.

The door swung open. In glided the painter, Robert Trenton. That stopped any further discussion.

He complemented his grey suit with a subtle silk tie. He had wingtip shoes like the pair William's dad had worn when he dressed up. His mother would have said it was the kind of taste money lets you wear.

"Hey, Harley, Paul. What's the damage, again, Emmett?" He pulled out his chequebook and pen, trying to act at ease with everyone. Like Brad, he wasn't convincing.

Harley whispered to William, "That's a Mont Blanc pen."

He figured she meant top of the line and expensive.

Trenton studied the invoice. "Right. That should cover it. Let me know when I can raise them." He wrote and tore the cheque out. "This should make her unbeatable."

Emmett bobbled his head in a noncommittal way. "Like I told you before, take five feet off the main boom and she'll handle better in strong winds."

Trenton spat out a laugh. "Well, I can't blame you for trying to help Daniel win."

He caught sight of William and that stopped him. "How many of us are racing?"

Harley said, "Daniel isn't registered, if that's what you want to know, Mr. Trenton."

Trenton suppressed a smile. "Ah, too bad. It's nice to win when the best are competing." When nobody answered, he nodded to Emmett and left.

"Were you really trying to make his boat go slower?" William whispered to Emmett.

"Nope. The man asks for advice but won't take it. What's the point of getting a dog if you're gonna do your own barking? He wants to win so badly he thinks we'd give him bad advice." The "he" and "we" painted Trenton as an outsider of sorts.

"He doesn't understand that a good race needs good competition. It's about getting the most out of your boat and crew, not just crossing the finish line first. When Daniel raced, he made everybody better because they brought their game up a notch."

Harley changed the topic. "Saw your boat out last week, Mr. Dingle — a beauty."

Dingle cracked a smile. "She is at that. By the way, Trenton is the odds-on favourite this year."

Emmett shook his head. "Dogs and the devil take us if he wins. He'll gloat forever."

Dingle lowered his voice. "Shall I put you down for your usual wager?"

Emmett scrunched his lips. "Not this year, Paul."

Harley said, "Stiff competition when Emmett finishes Trenton's new suit of sails."

"Speaking of sails, Emmett, I blew out one of my spinnakers. Can you …?"

"Of course, Paul. Anything else you need done?"

"No, the rest are well-made McCoy sails." He waved goodbye and strode out. Emmett and Harley dove on the sail bag he had brought in to examine the work to be done.

"Uh, Uncle Emmett, I wondered if you could use some extra help here in the shop."

Harley laughed. "Aren't sails a little old-fashioned for you?"

"I, uh, could use the money."

Emmett scratched his head. "Well, I don't know, everything's pretty specialized ..."

Harley jumped in. "C'mon, Grandpa, you could use a deckhand. Dingle's just given you some work." Emmett studied the sail's tear.

She slipped the cigar from the fish to the ashtray. "And Daniel might even enter the race like you want him to if William sails with him, right? So start him as a deckhand."

William's face fell. "A deckhand on the boat? On the water?"

"On the water is where we usually find boats, Master William."

By the time they'd closed the shop later that day, the breeze had freshened. Low tide uncovered a community of grey shore stones — grey, bald men sucking and floating water wisdom through beards of green algae. Their sightless faces contemplated the day's events as they had for so long, with a calmness he envied.

Small waves rocked Emmett's schooner, *Mary*, as it lay tethered to the dock. Except for the lack of a red jib, she was *Fathom*'s twin. Emmett and Harley sprang effortlessly onto her deck. His fear of water rooted William to the dock.

Emmett said, "The first thing I want you to do is remove that shackle from the sail. You'll need a marlinspike. Take mine." Emmett held out his knife.

William produced the knife he'd found. "I, uh, I have a marlinspike right here."

Emmett marvelled, "So *you* got Jack's rigging knife. We wondered where it had got to after the, um, accident." He leaned in to admire it. "Right proper it should go to his son."

William had one foot anchored to the dock. He struggled to force the other onto the deck of the boat. His stomach lurched. Perspiration beaded on his forehead. He pressed the point of the marlinspike in the small hole of the shackle pin and started to unscrew it. He tried to focus, but horrific images flooded his mind.

Water rose to the pickup's hood, hissing as it steamed away from the hot engine. The headlights prodded the ocean. His father hung over the wheel, his face twisted towards him. Copper-tasting fear coated William's mouth. Darkness swallowed the lights.

William's knees buckled. The knife splashed into the harbour. "Damn, damn, damn!"

"Damn near three fathoms of water is what you have between yourself and your knife right now," said Emmett as he leaned over the gunwale to peer into the water.

William fought to hold back tears. He couldn't believe he had just lost his father's knife — again. "I just can't deal with the ocean."

"The great-grandson of the Real McCoy can't 'deal' with the ocean? He'd keelhaul you for your lack of *seavoir faire*," tsked Emmett.

With a cry of frustration, William rushed from the dock. He clattered away on his bike in confusion and shame. He heard Harley admonish, "Grandpa, did you say 'keelhaul'? Really?"

William biked past a building. Its brass plaque caught his eye: *Robert Trenton, Real Estate Law, Mortgage Broker.* So the painter was also a lawyer. The parking lot had two spots marked *Trenton-Private.* One had a BMW convertible with FNSH LNE on its vanity plate. The bumper sticker read, *Keep Austin Weird.* Beside it was a glistening, new motorcycle. He wished he could jump on it and ride away from his problems.

Half an hour later, William coasted by the Trenton residence. He spied the trophy in its look-at-me window. Even from this distance he could see the new strip of silver on the bottom that identified it as his father's trophy.

A man in a security guard's uniform opened the gate for a nurse. She was on the road pushing a wheelchair carrying an old man with an oxygen mask.

William pulled abreast of them. The old man stared at him and pulled his mask off. How could a man with a nurse and guard have such yellow teeth? "Jack. Have you found the gold yet?" he wheezed. Too startled to answer, William kept pedalling.

William trudged up beside Daniel on the veranda, staring at the horizon.

"Granddad, look, I know you're bummed out, but we really have to talk. Mom and I have a problem — a disagreement. And I wish I … well, I wish you'd do something, anything, keelhaul me even, whatever that means."

Daniel bolted to his feet as if hit by lightning. "Keelhaul? KEELHAUL? Who said anything about keelhaul?" Startled by Daniel's outburst, William staggered backward.

Daniel narrowed his eyes. "What's going on with you?"

William stood his ground and shot back, "What's going on with *you*?"

"Lad, in this part of the world, we don't talk like that to our elders."

William stammered, "I, I … haven't seen much of my elders in this part of the world."

"Hmn. Be that as it may, I'm here now. Who said anything about keelhaul?"

"Uncle Emmett. Said that because I was afraid of water, I should be keelhauled."

"Nobody's going to keelhaul my grandson."

"Well, what does it mean, Granddad?"

Daniel grew gloomy. "It was an ancient form of maritime punishment. A sailor would be bound hand and foot and dragged beneath the keel. If he didn't drown, the barnacles on the hull would likely cut him to ribbons."

"Geez, I don't think I'm up for that, Granddad."

"It was only used in very rare occurrences — despite what Hollywood fiction writers pretend. A captain in the British navy needed every able-bodied sailor he could get. More likely to use the cat-o'-nine-tails — the whip — for discipline."

"Then why do people say 'keelhaul'?"

"It was meant to intimidate you. Nowadays, it's just a figure of speech." His granddad looked at him. "You want to stay here, did you say?"

"Mom and I, well, we're not exactly getting along." Daniel waited for more. William continued his answer with a sigh. "Mom works full-time now, see ..." He paused to make sure his grandfather was still listening.

"She took my son. She pushed him to work so hard, his heart gave out."

So this was the reason his mother and his granddad were distant. William might have snapped back at his granddad to defend his mother, but his granddad's tone was more sad than harsh. Besides, he'd had enough fighting for one day.

"Uh, actually the doctors at the hospital said Dad had a bad heart and worried too much about his work. Anyway, Mom's got this new friend. This guy who works with her, Brad. He's always around and, well, like, I don't think it's right, Dad being dead just a year now. So I wondered if I could stay with you."

All this information seemed to startle Daniel. William added something so his request wouldn't sound too big. "Just for a while, you know, a little while."

"Of course you're welcome to stay. You're my grandson. Mary's … doing something… Halifax, I think. But she'll be back tomorrow. We can talk to her tomorrow."

"Okay, thanks, Granddad. Staying here with you would be … really cool."

Daniel coughed. "For God's sake you should know better than to sit out here in your shirt sleeves. You'll freeze your tiller. Let's see what Emmett brought us for dinner."

Chapter Eleven

Death Benefits

Cape Islander: a fishing motor trawler designed early 1900s, strong and reliable

William woke the next morning, having slept better than any night since he'd arrived. His grandfather was re-energized and looked a lot more like the hero from the news footage. Plus, he had agreed that William could stay in Lunenburg.

Wearing his dad's rowing team jacket, William thumped down the stairs to the smell of coffee brewing. His grandfather looked up and stared at the jacket.

"It's cool this morning," William said to explain not having asked to wear it.

He slipped the jacket on a chair. Daniel touched it. "They all came for their captain's funeral you know — the whole rowing team. Flew in from ..." He waved his hand as if to cover a vast expanse of geography. His eyes wandered to the window above the sink. A smile gained a handhold on his heart. "Look, Mary's flowers are blooming."

William joined in his grandfather's pleasure. He could see the tips of four or five purple buds bursting through their green casings. Watering was paying off. "Granddad, why don't you sit in Granny's chair, beside the flowers? I'll bring you your coffee. Milk only, right?" His father had said how, as a boy, he'd enjoyed bringing Daniel his coffee.

Daniel's eyes crinkled with appreciation. "Yes, yes, right."

William carried the coffee out. His grandfather had pulled the chair from under the overhang so he could see the rhododendron bush and catch the sun's warming rays. William placed the coffee mug on the armrest. He realized for the first time in a long time that he felt like he belonged.

The clock on the wall at D & E Sailmakers read eleven o'clock. His grandmother was back from Halifax. She had asked that Daniel, Emmett, and Harley meet here. The spiky mast on "Bill's" model boat had snagged a few more unpaid invoices.

The mood in the room told him something serious was going on. So did the presence of the banker, Mr. Dingle.

Harley tottered under the weight of a big tray bearing a teapot and mugs. William got up to help. A shake of her head told him lifting something from the tray would upset its balance. She poured tea with honey and milk as the discussion flowed.

Mary sipped, then said, "I'm afraid we have a serious family situation to discuss."

"How so?" asked Daniel.

Mr. Dingle piped up. "It has to do with your mortgage, Daniel. You remember that you took out a mortgage on your house to help Jack finance his loft in Toronto?"

"Of course I do."

"Well, you didn't take life insurance coverage on the loan and you have to pay it back."

"Why don't we discuss it inside?" said Emmett, waving the adults into his private quarters.

William shot Harley a worried look. She tiptoed over to the closed door, laid her ear against it, and scrunched up her eyes to better hear through the thick door. William sidled over and did the same. They could only get snatches of the conversation and long bits of muffled mumbling. It depended on the level of the speaker and the traffic noises from outside.

Emmett broke the silence. "… had a number of orders but … you unable to come in, I farmed a lot of it out. Not sure … clients will come back … a lot of our business was due to your success in the race, Daniel. Every time you won, orders came pouring in. And last year …"

"… got to be one bank that will give us a mortgage," protested Daniel.

"That's what I have been trying to do in Halifax." Mary explained. "… Trenton's office turned us down … going back to Halifax … see other private mortgage companies … maybe get lucky." Nobody's tone of voice spoke of luck.

Dingle weighed in. "I wish I could do more, Daniel. After all these years … my hands are tied … managed to extend the due date by a month on compassionate grounds. That's a couple of weeks past the day of the race … think of what options you have."

William pieced together the facts: his grandparents couldn't get a mortgage so they'd have to sell the house. Because property values had dropped they wouldn't get much when they did sell. And because Daniel had been too upset to work full-time, they might also lose the sail loft. William couldn't breathe. The haven he had run away to was about to disappear.

Harley's breathing grew shallow. She bowed her head as if in prayer. She was vulnerable. Now he understood her eruption in the car, her hand on the building as though patting a friend goodbye. Along with worrying about Daniel and Mary's fate, she was worried about losing the loft, where she had played as a child and worked in her teens — a place where she was a regular.

They heard people shuffling towards them. Harley waved him over to the Scrabble game, which they pretended to play as the adults emerged sombre-faced. Mr. Dingle took his leave, Mary walking him out to his car.

Colour seemed to drain from Harley's face as she moved the dirty cups to the sink. Daniel made his way outside. He needed air.

William hurried outside and caught up to his granddad.

They walked on in silence a moment. William spoke in a small but firm voice. "We won't lose the house, Granddad — we won't."

William had no idea how this might come about. But something told him his grandfather had to get over his grief. And get back to sailing. And soon.

Chapter Twelve

The Real McCoy

Cutter: a boat carrying pilots or law enforcement officials

The day's events weighed heavily on all of them. Right after the meeting his grandmother had left for Halifax to seek a mortgage from private companies. His grandfather had barely touched dinner and retired early.

William had given some distance to the house and its sorrows by trudging down to think in *Fathom*'s cockpit.

The rain pelting the roof fought to be heard above the wind and the storm surge rasping the shore. The spindrift blowing in through the cracks couldn't keep him awake.

William's eyes fluttered open before he was fully awake. He pulled his jacket tighter against the chill. His eyes widened as he realized *Fathom* was under full sail. The same mysterious figure he had seen aboard the schooner with the red jib was at the helm.

"Hello, he's awake. Thought you were going to sleep right through our outing, my boy." A wave of the hand magically trimmed the sails, cranking them in tighter for maximum efficiency of sail shape to wind strength.

This wasn't his usual bad dream with his father sewing in the cockpit. The man in the cockpit wasn't even his father.

He was immediately taken by his size: well over six feet, shoulders that would make a wary person step aside on a sidewalk. The man's eyes were etched by a web of wrinkles probably from years of squinting on a bright ocean.

"You're the Real McCoy," offered William.

"As sure as your father was his father's son — and you, yours."

At least in this dream people answered when spoken to.

"I lost your knife. Dropped it in the harbour," William confessed.

McCoy nodded. "You might like to get that back. Use one of your father's old tricks. Tie a magnet on a fishing rod and dip 'er down till it bites. By the by, glad to see you're not frightened of the sea now, William."

"Well, it's a dream," reasoned William. "Where are we headed?"

McCoy motioned towards a point of land. "The island of Saint-Pierre. That's my old loading shed, where we used to load our liquor to sell in the States. She floats."

"Why a floating shed?"

"We usually used the main dock. But towards the end, we thought it best if the Coast Guard and the shore pirates didn't know when we loaded and when we left. We'd pull up at high tide, load up, and try to sneak out. Bullets, guts, and glory, my boy! Ah, well that's all in the past now. You know, Daniel could teach you a lot about sailing."

"Granddad's not teaching anything to anyone right now. He's like, like a ghost."

"I don't think you know much about ghosts."

"This is a weird dream."

"A dream — you're sure?" the Real McCoy challenged his conclusion.

"Well, I'm in the middle of the ocean, on a boat, talking to my dead great-grandfather."

"I'm not … exactly dead. Not in the usual sense."

"Yeah, right."

"I'm what's called an 'unsatisfied spirit.' In between two worlds, as it were."

"Why is that?"

McCoy sighed, "I'm stuck on my ship. Stuck till I make my peace with my son, your granddad. Till I give him something I've hidden for him — for the pain I caused him."

"Whad'ya hide?"

"Something of value."

"Yeah, what?" pressed William.

"You're presuming a certain degree of trust that hasn't been earned yet, lad. Tail that line, will you?"

"What? I don't know how to do that. Besides, you can sail magically, right?

"A lot could depend on your learning how to sail. Can you tie a bowline knot?"

"A what?"

"Man can't tie a bowline will never make it as a highliner."

"A high-what? Look, I don't know what you're talking about. But if you've got something of value, Granddad and Granny could do with some help. So, please, what did you hide?"

"I can only tell Daniel. But I will tell you that it was hidden down deep and that it floats up and down. And *Fathom* can take you there."

"This a riddle?"

"Life is a riddle. Important to get the clues right." McCoy stepped out of the cockpit to lean with his right arm lying loosely against the mast.

He stepped back into the cockpit. "Hang on." He pointed to the dubious-looking sails that bellied with wind. The boat whistled ahead, foaming at the bow as she slipped into wisps of fog. William felt as if he were floating. He hoped he wouldn't wake up.

From the stern, William heard the low roar of a motor. "Holy crap! Look at that."

A Coast Guard cutter rumbled out of the fog behind them.

"Let's make sure the Coast Guard boys don't knock at Daniel's door or there'll be the devil to pay." He waved his hand and the name *Fathom* magically became *Arethusa*.

A voice boomed over the loud-hailer. "Ahoy, *Arethusa*. This is Captain Thornton of the Coast Guard. You are operating without running lights. Heave to!"

McCoy whispered, "In the old days we'd burn oil-soaked rags, create a smokescreen, and turn around and come right along beside them. Nowadays, I mess up their radar." He pointed his hand in the cutter's direction.

Again the Captain's voice boomed through the loud-hailer. "Damn that radar. Keep your eyes peeled for that schooner on the starboard side!"

William grinned. "This is one cool dream."

McCoy kept his eye on the cutter. "Now we're going to give them the slip." And with a wave of McCoy's hand, his sails adjusted themselves effortlessly. The schooner passed on the cutter's port side. Two Coast Guard sailors buttoned their jackets against the cold that overtook them as *Fathom/Arethusa* glided into their wake.

"Ready about. Helm's down." McCoy gave a firm but quiet order.

"Which means what?" asked William, just as the swinging boom smacked his head.

Chapter Thirteen

Sleuth

Luff your sails: let the wind out of them to slow down

Streaks of morning light groped through cracks in the boathouse. They dappled William's sleeping form. He blinked sleep from his eyes and realized he was still in *Fathom*'s cockpit. He pulled himself upright and stared at an unfamiliar blanket covering him. He remembered falling asleep here but not covering himself with that blanket. The wind had died down. Above the sound of the waves washing the shore he could hear something *drip, drip, drip.*

He clambered down the ladder. His mouth fell open. Dripping seaweed clung to the keel. He rubbed the bruised bump on his forehead. He hadn't had a dream. He had been out on the ocean with the Real McCoy.

William crashed through the door at D & E Sailmakers. Harley held the cordless phone between her head and shoulder so she could enter data on the computer. She smiled and spread her fingers to let him know she'd be five more minutes. He spun around so she wouldn't see how desperate he was to tell her he'd seen a ghost. More importantly, would she believe him?

He had an idea. In the corner by the door sat an old barrel with a couple of fishing rods and two umbrellas. He skipped into the private quarters. He remembered the fridge door had magnets that held photos, bills, receipts, and the like. One was bigger. It was horseshoe-shaped with a small ring on top. That would be the one for the job.

Down at the dock William tied the magnet to the fishing line. He slid the magnet beneath the surface of the water where he figured he had dropped the knife, dunking it here and there. Lo and behold he raised two tin cans, four rusty bolts of different lengths, and, finally, the rigging knife. McCoy was right.

Back in the sail loft, Harley was off the phone. William launched into his explanation of his dream that wasn't a dream. It gushed out of him like a tide draining from a narrow inlet.

She was playing Scrabble against herself. The score sheet listed "me" and "me 2" as the players.

"Whoa, there, sailor. Luff your sails a bit."

"Huh?"

"Let some wind out of your sails and slow down."

"Why? Isn't that amazing? He's hidden something of value for Granddad!"

She noted his frown. "Oh, come on, Will, that's an awesome story. But you know … it's not like that actually happened. You know that, right? Maybe you were inspired by *Treasure Island.* Doesn't Jim Hawkins have problems at home and sail away in search of treasure?" She put down "rap" on the board for twelve points. "Didn't they think Ben Gunn was a ghost?"

"Ben Gunn wasn't dead. They only thought he was. So he wasn't a ghost. McCoy is dead, so I *was* sailing with a ghost."

William took letters from the second row of tiles. He spun the board, laid a "c" in front of her word, made "crap" and "catch" for thirty-six points.

"Mmhmm," she replied, keeping her eyes on her tiles.

William sucked in air and was about to bellow his indignation when the bell over the door clanged. He turned to see a Coast Guard captain stride in and remove his hat just as Emmett came down from the loft. Harley called out, "Morning, Captain Thornton."

"Louder and funnier, plea—" said Emmett until he caught sight of Captain Thornton.

"Emmett, any idea who might have been out in a schooner last night?" Thornton demanded.

"In that fog? A person would have to be daft." Emmett gave him an amused stare.

"There was a schooner that looked a lot like yours — except with a red jib. Any idea who that might be? Doesn't sound like anyone from 'round here, does it?"

"You catch her name?" Emmett's curiosity was aroused.

"Hard to read, but I thought it was *Arethusa*."

William poked Harley and gave her an I-told-you-so look.

Emmett chortled as he slipped the cigar from the ashtray back into the mounted fish head. "That's a good one. Someone's having you on, Captain. The *Arethusa* was the Real McCoy's rum-running boat. She ran aground near Sambro Shoal in, what was it, around 1929 — long after he'd sold it."

"Well, someone's going to have some explaining to do when we catch him. Good day, Emmett, Harley, young man?"

"William. William McCoy."

"Don't suppose you were out sailing a schooner with a red jib last night?" He smiled.

"Would you believe me if I said yes?" A big grin spread across the Captain's face as he left the shop.

William wasn't going to have an easy time of convincing people about his story. Emmett scooped two apples from the fruit bowl. He lobbed one to William and munched on the other as he plodded back up to the loft.

William grabbed Harley's arm. "That was us he was after," he hissed. "How do you think I got back this rigging knife you saw me drop in the harbour yesterday? McCoy told me to use a fishing line with a magnet on it."

She shrugged. "Wasn't there a story about Jack doing that to find Daniel's glasses?"

"Maybe. But how would I remember that? No, the Real McCoy got me to do it. Oh, and there was wet seaweed hanging from *Fathom*'s keel this morning. That's proof."

"There was a good blow last night. Wind coulda blown some kelp in through a crack in the boathouse," she reasoned.

He slumped into a chair. "Fathom" means to explain or understand, right?"

"Depends. A fathom is six feet. But it could also mean getting to the bottom of things, you know, like to figure something out. Is that your word?"

"No, but that's exactly what I've got to do."

McCoy had used terms that he knew vaguely. They seemed to have a double meaning, just like 'fathom.' If there was something "of value" out there that would help his grandparents, he needed to get the clues right and figure out the riddle.

"What's a highliner? I know Dad used it sometimes to mean somebody successful, right? Where does it come from?"

"You're asking about the difference between the literal and the figurative meaning of a word."

William spread his hands, palms up, in a what-are-you-talking-about gesture.

"Well," she began, "for example, when people say, 'there isn't enough room to swing a cat,' it literally means that there's not enough room to swing the whip called the cat-o'-nine-tails. Figuratively, it means space is tight."

"Yeah, okay, so what does 'highliner' mean, literally?"

"In the days of hook and line fishing, the doryman who caught the most fish was called a highliner. He would get the highest share of the sale of the schooner's catch. He's a good fisher. If someone tells you you're a highliner, it's like a compliment. Figuratively, it means success."

"Okay, and what's a bowline knot?" he asked, chomping on his apple.

Harley put down the word "sewing." "The king of knots. Why are you asking?"

"The Real McCoy said I should know how to tie one … and he also said he had something of value for Daniel."

She looked up at him. "Lots of rumours floating around about McCoy. Including money and murder —"

"Murder?" So there was some truth to what his granddad had said. He wasn't just rambling.

"Yes, a fisherman who used to work for McCoy was found shot. Can't remember all the details, just that when McCoy came back here before he died, he was supposed to have brought money. Some thought the money was the cause for the murder. That was a long time ago. Maybe you just heard one of those rumours …"

"I wasn't sailing with a rumour. And if Granddad inherits something of value, then he'd be able to keep his house. You've gotta believe me and help us."

Harley rolled her eyes. "If we're going on a guilt trip, Will, let me pack my bags." She looked into his pleading face. "I'm a journalist — or at least a soon-to-be journalist — and the first rule of any good story is to check your facts. So become a sleuth and find some." Her gaze roamed around the loft. "Who knows, if you do find something of value then Daniel might be able to keep his house … and the loft."

"How do you start checking out a ghost?"

"Well, don't ask people about a ghost or they'll think Toronto boy's gone soft in the head. Start with asking about his boat. Everybody around here likes talking about boats. You might start with Manny at Manny's Grill." She pushed over a spiral notepad and a pen.

"Manny?"

"Yes, Manny is kind of the keeper of the tales around here. Everybody talks to him. And he volunteers at the Maritime Museum. See what he says."

He nodded and left. He didn't tell her that he'd already met Manny.

Chapter Fourteen

Dead Man's Tale

Tancook schooner: a schooner designed and made on Tancook Island, N.S.

Manny called it the mid-morning lull, after breakfast and before lunch. He sat on the counter, his head tilted back. As if the answer he was looking for was on the ceiling.

"The rumours about the murder involved a fisherman called Cavendish. There was bad blood between McCoy and Cavendish. In some people's minds, finding McCoy's raccoon coat with blood on it linked McCoy to the death."

"Was McCoy charged with murder?"

"Nope, never was."

Four early lunch customers burst into Manny's Grill, clamouring for his attention.

"Gotta get back to work. Why don't you go to the Roué Reading Room at the library just around the corner. On Pelham Street. Look at what they've got. Ask for Marianne." Manny pointed to Pelham Street on another map of downtown Lunenburg on his paper placemats.

William had also wanted to ask Manny if there was talk of gold linked to McCoy because of old Mr. Trenton's question about it.

Maybe it was just crazy talk. Either way, Manny was too busy to discuss it right now.

Marianne had brown hair with purple-red ends. A lambskin vest topped her green plaid skirt and her smile flashed matching green braces.

"A lot of rum-runners had to hire captains and boats. McCoy, on the other hand, was a first-class sailor with his own boat. When he retired, McCoy bought a Tancook schooner and converted it from fishing boat to blue-water sailor — a pleasure craft. The Tancook schooners were the inspiration for the *Bluenose.*"

She pointed a red fingernail towards photographs and plaques on the walls. She explained that the Mr. Roué for whom the reading room had been named had designed the famous *Bluenose*. She pointed to a model of the schooner that sat in a small recess between two photographs of Mr. Roué. Apparently, in the early 1900s, *Bluenose* was the fastest fishing schooner of its day. And getting your catch to market fast, she explained, meant getting the best price. Looking at it in miniature, William realized that it looked a lot like *Fathom* when he'd seen it sitting in its cradle in the boathouse.

The librarian continued. "The fisherman from Gloucester, Massachusetts, sent a challenge to all fishing schooners from New England and the Maritimes. They wanted to race. Angus Walters from Lunenburg, the captain of *Bluenose*, won more times than any other boat or captain." She nodded for emphasis. William jotted down some notes. He liked history but he was more interested in whether McCoy had hidden some gold.

"If you want more information, try the Old Lunenburg Historical Society." She circled their location on William's map.

The archivist for the Old Lunenburg Historical Society blinked through thick, oversized glasses. His blinking and his hairy ears made him look like an owl. He spoke from behind his desk. "Yes, we have all sorts of things on the Real McCoy on our computers upstairs. But access is restricted to people doing scholarly research. Do you have a letter from your teacher confirming this?"

William stomped out and down to the sidewalk. He stopped, turned, and studied the building. Between the buildings he spotted a drainpipe leading up to a second-floor window. He slipped into the passageway and tugged on the drainpipe. It was secure. He tucked the notebook under his belt and shimmied up the pipe.

He flattened against the wall and held his breath. A woman pushed a baby stroller along the path beneath him. He held his breath till she passed without looking up. He reached for the window, which was open a crack, and pushed it wide enough to slide in.

A tap of the keyboard roused the computer. They obviously didn't need a password, what with the owl standing guard downstairs. He scanned articles and took notes. He found some old newspaper photographs showing McCoy arriving at the Halifax train station in the fall of 1947. His full-length raccoon coat flapped open to show his initials on the lining. McCoy didn't look too happy to be greeted by the press. What was he trying to keep out of the papers?

There was a photo taken a few weeks later of a fisher called Cavendish, "shot in the chest with a large bore revolver on his Cape Islander." There was a close-up of Cavendish's face that showed a faint indentation under his cheekbone. It was a crescent moon with a star at either end. There was also one of McCoy's bloodstained raccoon coat with the initials "W.M." on the lining, found on the beach a few miles from the body.

William heard voices. The owl-faced man invited the visitor he called professor to use the empty research room. William hit "print" as he heard the visitor start up the stairs. He jammed a chair against the door. The first photo came off the copier just as the visitor tried the door and called to say it was locked.

"What?" he hooted. "I unlocked everything when I came in."

The second picture appeared on the tray. The third started printing as William heard keys jangling up the stairs. William scooped up the last picture, moved the chair, and scampered out the window. The door creaked open just as he pulled his leg out. The owl-faced man was talking to the visitor. He didn't see William fleeing.

He slithered down the drainpipe, catching his knee on a bracket, and bit his lip. He rubbed his knee then reread his notes as he limped back to the sail shop.

Rum-running was a risky, exciting occupation. And it was profitable. An RCMP officer made about seventy-five dollars a month at that time, while a rum-runner could make three hundred. A captain who owned his boat like McCoy made a whole lot more.

He bounded into the sail loft and slapped his notebook down between the computer and cash register. That got Harley's attention. "You wanted facts? Fifty thousand dollars was missing from the Real McCoy's estate when he died in Florida. They think he brought it with him and hid it in Lunenburg. Cool, huh?"

"That sounds like a lot of money. Did he earn enough for that to be possible?"

William opened his hands, palms up, to say he didn't know.

"Oh, your mom called. She was sorry she missed you."

"Yeah? Was Brad there?" His tone was cold.

Harley shrugged. Without asking if he was hungry she skipped into the kitchen. She ladled out a bowl of soup and brought it back out for him. "She said she'd call you again." Harley could see that her cousin was troubled. She picked up the notebook and said, "Why don't we talk to Manny at the Fisheries Museum tomorrow? A couple of times a week he does the afternoon talk on rum-runners. I'll eat lunch late and come with you. This still doesn't mean I believe in all this ghost stuff, though."

William studied the Scrabble board and turned "ant" into "phantom." "But you'd like me to find 'something of value,' right?"

"Well, duh ...," she answered, which got them both laughing.

The next day they headed to the museum, munching on Harley's sandwiches. Between the wharf and the road stood a circle of black obelisks.

He knew what they were because his parents had a photo of themselves in Place de la Concorde in Paris — the photo his mom had removed from their pin board. In it they stood beside a big obelisk Napoleon had brought from his conquest of Egypt.

The obelisk in the middle of this cluster had a carved inscription: *Dedicated to the memory of those who have gone down to the sea in ships and who have never returned.* Even with the sun shining on them they looked as dark as the water they spoke of.

He had slowed down, and Harley mistook his change of speed as interest. She told William the story of the family names engraved on the black granite obelisks. "When the August gales came up, well, some of those storms wiped out entire families. That's why they passed a law that stopped all the men — fathers and sons — of the same family from sailing together on the same ship. So women weren't left destitute."

Harley stopped and touched the names of four family members who had perished on the same voyage in 1927. "If these four men had lived, their great-grandchildren would have been our cousins. Granddad Emmett says that the seas roar during a storm to mask the screams of dying sailors. Sometimes, when you go to sea, there's the devil to pay. You know where that expression comes from, Toronto boy?"

"It's about being in trouble, but I don't know where it comes from."

"Well, it's not the devil with the horns. On the old boats they filled the seams between deck planks with oakum. That's a type of coarse fibre and that was called 'paying.' Hot tar would seal the oakum. The farthest seam out was called 'the devil' because it gave you a devil of a time to seal it. So, like, the full expression is, 'the devil to pay and no pitch hot' — no hot tar to pour over the oakum. It means that you have a difficult task, or a lot of grief. Going to sea during the August gales was a big challenge. All these names on the obelisks prove that."

They got to Manny's just as he was closing and walked together to the museum.

"Hey, Manny, how's it going?" Harley asked. "You've met my cousin, William?"

"I've had the pleasure," said Manny with a bob of his head.

"You believe in ghosts, Manny?" asked Harley to William's embarrassment.

He gave Harley a serious look without breaking pace. "I don't mess with ghosts."

William smiled. Finally he had an ally.

"My ancestors," continued Manny, "came from Africville, outside of Halifax. 'Fore that they was runaway slaves. Come up from the States on the Underground Railroad. And 'fore that, they was shipped from Benin in Africa, where there's a long history of believing in spirits, hougans, and zombies. So, yes, I believe in ghosts. Why you askin'?"

"William thinks he saw a ghost," said Harley.

Manny stopped at the museum door. "Seeing a ghost usually means something's afoot … something's going to happen."

Chapter Fifteen

A Secret to Die For

Taffrail: the rail at the stern of a boat

William didn't know the rum-runner's world, so he intended to listen to Manny with the hope he'd tell them something to solve McCoy's "up and down" riddle.

William did know that there were differences between Canadian and American Prohibition — the banning of alcohol. Canada's started as part of the 1914 War Measures Act in order to save grain and fruits for the population. At the end of the war each province chose when to repeal Prohibition.

The American Prohibition was intended to stop men from drinking away a family's income. And from not showing up for work. Republican Andrew Volstead got Congress to pass the Volstead Act, which, despite a presidential veto, took effect January 16, 1920.

"How could rum-runners buy alcohol here during our prohibition?" asked William.

Manny took a breath before answering. "A good question. Our prohibition wasn't as restrictive as the American one. Americans were not allowed to make, transport, or consume alcoholic beverages. We couldn't drink, but we could distill and brew for export."

"When did the Americans start drinking again?" asked William.

Manny gave him a sly smile. "Officially? Officially they didn't repeal Prohibition till they passed the Twenty-first Amendment on December 5, 1933. And they did that because poisonous home-brews blinded and killed people. It also led to gangsterism that shot and killed people, not to mention untaxed profits."

Profits! That's what William wanted to know about. Harley had her own question.

"So you're saying that Americans and Canadians were breaking the law?"

"Best ways to 'splain this," began Manny, "is to quote McCoy, who said that the law was unquestionably the law but morality was a personal choice. Americans got a long tradition of fighting laws they found wrong-minded, like the tea tax and the runaway slave law."

"How is Nova Scotia connected?"

"They would buy their alcohol to smuggle, some from Europe but mostly from Canada, the Bahamas, or the French island of Saint-Pierre. It was the Real McCoy who brought prosperity to Saint-Pierre when Halifax had refused to refit his schooner *Arethusa* in 1921. He spent his money there on gear and started buying some of his alcohol there."

"You said rum-running was big here in Nova Scotia?" prodded William. He wanted to know whether McCoy could have brought $50,000 with him back to Lunenburg.

"Nova Scotia was the best place to buy Scotch. Halifax, the city that had refused to let McCoy refit his schooner a year earlier, now saw the financial merit of doing business with him. So this province became a favourite port of call."

"Why is that?" asked Harley.

"Scotch whisky from Halifax cost him only $12 a case, and he didn't pay duty here like he did in the Bahamas."

"You mean he paid duty to governments when he ran alcohol?" Harley interjected.

"Oh, yes. They said he was a straight man in a crooked world. He would pay the Bahamian government somewheres around $30,000 in customs fees."

William was skeptical. "Well, if he was paying that kind of money in duty, how did he make a profit? I mean $30,000 was a lot of money in those days."

Manny nodded. "McCoy would load *Arethusa* for around $150,000. He'd sell his load for over $300,000."

"So how much money did McCoy make?" William pressed.

"His profits went up and down." William's ears pricked up at that phrase.

"McCoy had to pay for refitting fees — the Atlantic was hard on a boat. He had to pay for weapons. And for lawyers to get him out of jail."

"McCoy went to jail?" William hadn't heard that before.

Manny nodded. "What sunk McCoy was a handwritten note giving one of his captains explicit directions on where to take the cargo. McCoy learned his lesson. From then on he either didn't write notes or used cryptic expressions to confuse the authorities."

"Like a riddle?"

"Yes, like a riddle — but one his crew would get."

And like the one McCoy had given William about "up and down." "You mentioned weapons. Was that to do with the murder of the fisher called Cavendish?"

"McCoy bought First World War surplus Thompson machine guns and shotguns, which he kept handy in the furled part of the sail when doing business on Rum Row. His crew knew how to use them too. Most were Royal Canadian Navy veterans.

"Why did he need guns?" asked William.

"Shore pirates would raid ships waiting to unload at Rum Row. But McCoy only had weapons for defence. There's no proof he ever shot anyone or killed anyone."

"What about Cavendish?"

"McCoy was never charged. That death occurred in 1947, more than fifteen years after Prohibition was repealed."

William caught himself tapping his fingers against his pants. He was getting closer.

Manny glanced at his watch. "And that, ladies and gentlemen, is the end of the guided portion of your visit. Please feel free to wander through the exhibits. Thank you."

The tourists applauded their appreciation, then shuffled off in small groups.

Manny left the museum with William and Harley in tow.

"Any idea how much money McCoy actually made?" William squinted in the sun.

"Or did he drink most of his profits?" mused Harley.

"Nope. McCoy was a Methodist teetotaller. He said he preferred blue water to firewater. Drank very rarely. In fact, he once said that after his death, his ghost might keep right on, like the *Flying Dutchman*, to warn people to obey the laws of Prohibition."

At the mention of a ghost, William nudged Harley.

"So he made a lot of money?" asked William.

"Well, he retired with a modest amount of money. Nobody actually knows how much for sure. He worked hard from 1920 to about 1925. After that gangsters like Capone got into the business. It got rougher, dirtier, and wasn't fun for him. So he bought a Tancook schooner and retired."

"What about the money he was supposed to have brought here in 1947?"

"Lots of rumours about the gold McCoy supposedly brought back from Saint-Pierre."

William was confused. "I thought it was money — you're saying it was gold?"

"I'm saying that was the rumour. Started a kind of gold rush here in 1947, just before he died. That lasted almost five years. Lots of folks looking for it. Looking hard, digging up everybody's backyard. Never found a thing."

Was this the gold that old Mr. Trenton in the wheelchair was asking about?

Manny led them down a back alley that serviced a number of businesses. He stopped by a sign by a door that read *Taffrail Pub. Staff Parking Only.* Tidy, empty, aluminum beer kegs and garbage bins flanked both sides of the door. Manny waved them in.

"You work here?" William asked as he let the screen door slam behind him.

"Own it with a partner. It's only breakfast and lunch at the grill. So I do the paperwork for this place. Get to watch sports on the big screen."

Manny gestured for them to sit on a couch in what looked like a back office. Plaques on the walls celebrated Manny's volunteer work. They hung with a series of baseball players William didn't recognize, but he knew enough to know they were professionals. Some showed Manny, a much younger Manny, in different uniforms. One of the frames quoted a saying that seemed to sum up the quiet man Manny was: *If you win, say little. If you lose, say less.*

Manny opened a little fridge and pulled out three cans of fruit juice. He tossed them each one. He snicked the top off his before tilting his head back and glugging a long draught down his throat.

Harley brought them back to McCoy. "What started the rumours of gold?"

"They say that in 1947 McCoy arrived with a doctor's satchel made of alligator leather full of rum-running money. He was from

Florida. Lots of 'gators there. He bought a Tancook schooner and sailed to Saint-Pierre before coming back to Lunenburg. When he came back from Saint-Pierre and unloaded his boat, he didn't have his alligator bag anymore."

William pulled out the photocopies he'd made at the historical society. He showed them the one of McCoy wearing a raccoon coat and carrying an alligator skin doctor's bag, then the pictures of Cavendish's body. "Who was this guy, Cavendish?"

"Cavendish was a big, tough veteran from the Royal Canadian Navy. From all accounts a good sailor but a mean drunk. He'd go ashore and start fights in bars, including with his own shipmates. So McCoy let him go. Cavendish said he'd get even with McCoy, even though he paid Cavendish all he owed him plus a bonus."

Manny pointed to the island of Saint-Pierre on a wall map. "Word from Saint-Pierre was that a lot of gold changed hands. It would be worth more than a million dollars today. He had many friends in Saint-Pierre, made a lot of them rich. Cavendish was killed after McCoy came back from Saint-Pierre."

What, wondered William, happened to the alligator bag with the money?

Chapter Sixteen

Sea Legs

Dacron: synthetic material used for sails

Back at the loft, William flipped through his notes. "Manny said the Real McCoy bought alcohol from Saint-Pierre. And I know he operated from a floating boat shed to avoid detection." He studied a map of the eastern seaboard.

Harley looked at him skeptically. "And you know this … from your dream?"

"Here! Right here. I saw it. It floats 'up and down.' This is where the gold is!"

"Well then I guess if we want to find it, we have to sail to Saint-Pierre."

"You mean … sail, like, on a sailboat?"

"Hey, if you did go on the boat with the Real McCoy, then you've proven you can do it. Or was that all just stuff you made up?"

"No, I … I …"

"Listen, I know why you're afraid of the water, with the accident. I get it. But Emmett said you used to swim like a fish."

He put down "drown" on the scrabble board. She put an "s" on the end to make "safe" and said, "Fear is something we all deal with."

"Yeah, right. You're not afraid of anything."

"Heights. I'm afraid of heights."

William made a face and pointed to a photo of Harley hoisted to the top of a mast.

"The trick, Will, is you got to look your fear in the eye. You won't conquer it but it won't intimidate you so much. I hold my breath and stare at the mast the whole way up."

He mulled this over.

"And losing this place. That … well, I'd gladly be hoisted aloft the tallest mast a dozen times rather than risk that." She took a moment. "If you go, I'll teach you the bowline knot. So you can impress the Real McCoy next time you see him." She winked at him.

"I want to … it's just that I … when I'm near water, I see my father there …"

"Will, the boat's in the water, you're not." Then an idea came to her. She pulled out her measuring tape and took William's measurements. "You work on that — that fear of water." She opened a cupboard marked "Odds and Ends" and pulled out scraps of Dacron. "And I'll work on keeping you in the boat."

They heard footsteps on the stairs.

"Here comes Emmett. Why don't we ask him about Saint-Pierre?"

Harley broached the topic first.

Emmett slipped the cigar back into the fish's mouth. "Saint-Pierre? Take too long, right, Frank the Fish? The best racers do it in fifty-some hours — with a prevailing wind. We don't have time to get there and back in a reasonable amount of time." He studied the words they'd made on the board.

"Getting there isn't as important as getting Will on the boat."

"Okay … but why Saint-Pierre?" He leaned over the Scrabble board.

William said, "I've got this ... thing about the island. We, uh, we studied it in class."

"I'm sure you studied the moon but it doesn't mean we're going there."

Harley joined in. "It'll, uh, give me a topic for my university entrance essay."

Emmett studied the two cousins, then used the "f" from "safe" to make "fart." "Why do I think I'm being lied to?"

"No, we're not lying. It's just that we're teenagers, and, well, it just sounds like a lie."

"Well, 'sounds like a lie' is what I said."

"Then we agree," she said, smiling. Emmett rolled his eyes. Harley slipped the cigar from the fish's mouth to the ashtray.

"Dogs and the devil," muttered Emmett.

"Grandpa, you said that Daniel was more likely to race with Will."

"No, Harley, you said that."

"But you agreed." Emmett chewed on this. "See, Grandpa? This is perfect for Daniel and Will. And I bet you Will and I will make a great team."

Emmett looked almost convinced.

After Emmett left, the cousins gave each other a high five. They were one step closer to sailing for Saint-Pierre and gold.

Chapter Seventeen

The Island of Saint-Pierre

Bollard: a substantial pillar to which a boat is secured, usually dockside

Sunrise found William pacing the dock beside Emmett's schooner. He stared at the bits of harbour debris, floating to make you forget that most things drowned or sank in the ocean. Leaning against the bollard, he raised his leg towards the deck. A wave slapped between the hull and the dock and staggered him. Memories flooded back.

Dark ocean water invaded the pickup, swirled around his father's open eyes, and moved his hair in a goodbye wave.

He shook his head, closed his eyes, and repeated, "The boat's in the water, I'm not." He pocketed the rigging knife and jumped onto her bobbing deck.

With a thud, Harley's duffel landed on *Mary*'s deck. She looked at him, curled up by the mast, his rigging knife clutched like a talisman. They smiled.

Harley pulled her masterpiece from a sail bag — a harness made with a Dacron-shrouded life jacket with a well-reinforced stainless steel U-hook protruding out front. She nodded for him to put it on.

William asked, "Will Granddad be okay on his own for a while?"

"Got a neighbour looking in. Your grandma's back soon."

Emmett sprang aboard. He studied her harness. "Wow, what are you anchoring, an elephant?"

"A dream. William's dream," answered Harley.

"You believe in it?"

"It's his dream. And he's trying to make it work, which is the important thing, right?"

"Man should have a dream," Emmett concluded with a nod to William.

Harley took a twenty-foot line and whipped a bowline knot at either end of the rope. The first coiled around the main mast, the second through the hook on his harness. "The king of knots. It won't slip and, like, cut you in half if you're pulled up a mast or through water, but you can undo it with just a flip of the wrist. Provided it's not under tension." She flipped the top of the line to free the knot. She retied the knot with a mantra: "The rabbit comes up the hole, around the tree, and back down the hole."

William looked at his cousin and realized he didn't mind wearing clothes from someone this cool.

She added, "You can get anywhere you need to on the boat with this length of rope. Except probably the head. You'll have to undo it if you need to go ..." Their smiles grew to a laugh as he imagined himself fighting the rope to get to the boat's toilet.

When she had stopped laughing, she asked him if he knew why it was called a head.

"Uh-uh," he answered.

"In the early days of sailboats, the 'seat of ease,' as it was called, was at the head of the boat, near the bottom of the bowsprit so the ocean's waves could clean it."

Emmett motored out of the bay, towing a tender behind.

"Why are we towing a lifeboat?" William asked nervously.

"It's a tender so we can row to locations too shallow for *Mary*'s six-foot keel."

William and Harley hoisted the sails, hand over hand, and secured lines to belaying pins. Emmett killed the diesel. The boat heeled over in the freshening breeze. William clung to the rigging.

Harley and Emmett exchanged a look and launched into a bit of history. William knew it was meant to distract him and was glad for it.

"Not surprising McCoy bought some of his boats and refitted them here. Lunenburg employed a number of really good carpenters to build its fleet of wooden schooners. Those carpenters also built some fine-looking houses for those captains and merchants who got rich at sea." She pointed to the old houses that dotted the old town and harbour.

"They got rich just from fishing?"

Emmett shook his head no. "They fished the Grand Banks of Newfoundland in the fall, then traded salted cod for rum and molasses in the Caribbean in the summer. Some also got into rum-running in the twenties. But for decades it was about fishing and trading." Emmett went below.

"How old is this place?" he asked Harley.

"Well, the British wanted to get rid of Acadian settlers who were faithful to the French king. They invited anyone who wasn't Catholic. About fourteen hundred settlers arrived in 1753. That's how we ended up with so many Germans and Huguenots from the area of Montbéliard in France who wanted to escape persecution by the Catholics." Her ease at the helm allowed William to relax as they made for open water.

Emmett came up and unfurled a chart. He showed them where they were and where they were heading — a lot of open water to cross.

Hunkered safely in the cockpit, William practised tying the bowline. Emmett showed him which line did what to which sail and how to cleat a line to secure it temporarily or permanently with more figure eights around the T-shaped metal fixed to the deck. He showed him how to pull lines clockwise around the winches. To tighten the sails to maximum efficiency, Emmett slid a winch handle in place and cranked it. William understood that a winch allowed a sailor enough strength to offset the power of a full sail.

The sun set on the ocean, a big orange ball melting into the water. Emmett watched as William tied a leather lanyard to the knife and to his belt using bowline knots.

"How on earth did you get that knife back?" marvelled Emmett.

"I, uh, I uh ..."

"In plain English now, William. No bilge water."

"I used a, a magnet on a fishing pole." He omitted the idea had come from a ghost.

Emmett beamed. "You clever, clever boy ... Listen, I know you're afraid. Only a stupid man says he's never afraid. You know how a sailboat works?"

William nodded. "It's powered by wind."

"Right you are. Under normal conditions a good design and a good sailor will not let the wind overpower the boat and tip it or broach it." He used his hand as the sail. His forearm took the place of the keel. "As wind comes from windward, sails fill and propel the boat forward. That same force heels the boat over, allowing the excess wind to spill out. And the weight of the keel underwater helps keep that balance, even if the lee rail is underwater. Windward, leeward," he added pointing to show that windward meant the side the wind was coming from and the lee was where the wind was headed. "You understand?"

"Yes, but …"

"Sometimes it takes a while for emotions to catch up to our understanding. Keep an eye on these." He pointed to fluttering strings tied to the stays. "They're telltales. They tell the tale of the wind, its direction and strength, how well the sail is shaped. They're telling us this steady breeze is nothing to worry any of us." William believed him.

The stars marked their path through the two-foot swells. William, secure in his harness, stood at the helm. Emmett was sleeping below. Harley, a solo helmsman since her early teens, tethered the wheel to its present course by means of two short lines slipped over two of the wheel's spindles with the other ends secured to either side of the cockpit. She gestured for William to stand behind the wheel and she lay on the banquette.

"That'll hold our course, William. I really have to close my eyes for a few minutes. Sewed late last night. Wake me if anything happens. And I mean anything."

A while later William, lulled by the soothing motion of the boat, caught himself nodding off. He jumped when the Real McCoy pulled *Fathom* alongside. William put his index finger to his lips so they wouldn't wake Harley. He untied his safety hook, then quickly whipped the bowline knot back on and beamed at his newfound competence. The Real McCoy gave him a thumbs-up, then filled Emmett's sails.

They surged over a great distance, the lee rail canting so much it cut through the top of waves. William pulled a blanket over Harley.

Emmett checked their position and was stunned at their progress. Before them lay Saint-Pierre. He tapped the GPS and checked again. The reading remained the same. McCoy's old loading shed came into view. It looked a lot more decrepit than it did at night. Its cedar planks were weathered all silver, some were missing, and it listed to a side like an old man with back problems.

Chunk, chunk, chunk, grated the anchor chain chaffing its way through its hawse hole to the ocean floor. Harley showed William how to secure the sails by lashing them to their booms as the *Mary* swung lazily at anchor.

Emmett shielded his eyes to study his two mastheads and the stays that secured them to various points on the boat. "Harley, would you go up in the bosun's chair and check the rigging? Took a strong wind to get us here this quickly. Let's make sure nothing was stressed or damaged."

She took a deep breath and gave William a nod to show that she was fighting her fears. Harley produced the bosun's chair, a series of straps that fitted around her thighs and back. Emmett undid the line from the mainsail and secured it to the steel ring on Harley's straps. A backup line from the main mast was also fitted to the steel ring.

Emmett ran the spare line around one of the belaying pins. He did it in a figure eight over the top and bottom of the pin, then the last loop was flipped over on itself to lock it in place. William remembered a drawing of a pirate in *Treasure Island* using the stout, foot-long belaying pin as a weapon. Emmett showed him how to let the safety line feed up while providing a safety brake should the main line fail. Emmett cranked Harley up using the winch.

"What did you call that?" asked William.

"A bosun's chair," answered Emmett. "The name comes from 'boatswain.' He was the petty officer in charge of the rigging crew on a ship." He was panting by the time he had cranked Harley to the top. She asked him to lower her a bit. Emmett uncoiled a wrap from the winch and slid the coils backward so Harley could look at the spreaders. They pushed the stays outward as they came down to the deck, allowing someone to walk beneath them.

When she said everything looked good, they lowered her to the deck, where she gave out a breath of relief.

"And that's how you get up and down a mast," commented Emmett.

"Up and down," there was that phrase again. In case he was missing something, William offered to go up the second mast. They hoisted him in the bosun's chair so he could look for signs of stress, wear, and breakage. There being none, he enjoyed the pendulum effect cause by the boat's gentle rocking. He was tipped from this side to that but wasn't afraid. From his perch he saw the French *tricolore* flag fluttering above a distant house.

William studied the shed, which listed to one side but refused to topple.

Emmett pulled the tender alongside so they could climb in. William stalled and Emmett rolled his eyes. "Jaysus Murphy. Look over there, William. You can see bottom right beside the shed. You can probably stand — no more than waist-deep. We can't wait for the tide to come in and moor up against the shed."

William felt Harley's steadying hand on his shoulder. "The boat's in the water, I'm not," murmured William, as he scampered down the ladder to the tender. That's when Harley thought to explain the real purpose of their trip.

"You mean the Real McCoy's money?" thundered Emmett. "I should have known. Those were nothing but rumours started by a bunch of, of reprobates. Dogs and the devil. Listen, if there were riches to be found, it would have been found by now."

"Calm down, Grandpa. What's the harm here? Would it be so bad to find McCoy's money and a chance to save the loft?"

Emmett made a face but gestured for Harley to keep rowing.

William tied the painter, the tender's tethering rope, to the shed and stripped off his harness. Emmett and Harley followed, careful to walk on the beams.

"So it's either cash in a doctor's bag, or it's gold," William reminded the others.

"Ya don't take Visa?" Emmett smirked. Laughter overtook them.

Remnants of American and French flags hung on the walls. The ocean bottom was visible through missing floorboards. Emmett dropped knee-deep into the shallow water and checked the underside of the floating shed but found nothing.

At the top of the loft, Harley's search yielded an old table and chairs. Emmett tapped his watch to indicate it was nearing time for them to leave. He didn't believe they'd get as favourable a wind going back as they did coming. And he didn't want to leave Daniel alone for too long.

Desperate, William tapped on the walls with the butt-end of his rigging knife, holding his ear to the boards, till he got a hollow response. Harley and Emmett hurried over.

Emmett took William's knife and prodded the boards with the marlinspike until a secret panel creaked open. He retrieved a dusty deck of cards and an old bottle that looked like a champagne bottle with the remnants of a black seal and a cork. He pulled the cork, sniffed it, then took a swig of rum and sighed contentedly. William explored the space and scooped out a mouldy doctor's bag.

He scraped away the mould to reveal alligator skin. Manny's story had been right. Wide-eyed, they gathered around as William opened the case. Empty! Angry, he swung it towards the wall, ripping the handle from the case. An American hundred-dollar bill dated 1946 floated down from where it had been wedged all these years.

Chapter Eighteen

The Wishing Well

Tender: small boat that services a larger boat at mooring or dock

Jim Hawkins, the hero of *Treasure Island*, sailed home on the *Hispaniola* with his gold. William wasn't having the same luck on *Mary*.

"If it's any consolation, lad, you're not the only one to be taken in by those rumours about the money," Emmett said, trying to make the best of a disappointing day.

William yanked out the handle of the doctor's satchel and held it up. "No! They weren't rumours. This is the handle to the alligator case he carried his money in. I'm certain that this is the last of the money he had in it." William unfolded the hundred-dollar bill and weighed it down with his knife. He pulled out the black and white photo of McCoy. "This is a photo of McCoy arriving in Halifax with the satchel in hand and wearing the raccoon coat that was found on shore and all bloody right after Cavendish was murdered." William caught his breath. "In plain English, Uncle Emmett, the gold or the money did exist. We just haven't found it yet."

"I have to tell you that if I caught those reprobates who started those rumours, I'd give them a piece of my mind. Wasted a lot of people's time. Like ours."

Harley saw William's disappointment. "Grandpa, if I weren't so tired, I'd, I'd … I'd give you a piece of my mind. Remind me to do that in the morning."

"And if I forget?"

"If you forget … well, then I'll, I'll … give you a piece of my mind."

"A win-win proposition," said Emmett.

She gave him a peck on the cheek and headed below to her berth.

William started to follow his cousin below deck but Emmett's "come here" wave brought him back to the cockpit. "See this?" asked Emmett, holding up the bottle of rum they'd found. "This is what people argued about for so long." William took the bottle and smelled the strong amber liquid and made a face. He breathed ocean air to soothe his nostrils and throat.

"At some point your grandmother will likely offer you a little glass of wine with water in it. That way when your young friends produce a bottle they've stolen from their parents it won't hold the attraction of forbidden fruit. Moderation in all things is a lesson your father would have been proud to teach you … just as Daniel taught him. Turn in if you like. I'll stand first watch."

William settled in on the opposite banquette. "I think I'll just stay up here with you for a while, if that's okay."

Emmett seemed pleased. The two settled into quiet companionship. William was happy that Emmett had taken the time to show him that he was safe on a sailboat.

The next morning, Emmett came up through the hatch, blinking at the sunlight. According to the GPS, they were once again way ahead of schedule and coming up to the coast of Nova Scotia. "I've heard of favourable wind, but … nothing like this," he marvelled from below.

William, safe in his harness, practised tying a bowline knot with a length of rope around his midriff. His face, hair, and hands were wet with ocean spray.

William was at the helm when Emmett carried his coffee on deck.

"How come this schooner is identical to *Fathom*?" William asked. Emmett shot him a quizzical look. William added quickly, "I saw *Fathom* in the boathouse below Granddad's house."

Emmett took a long gulp of coffee and let out a sigh. "They're both Tancook schooners — made by the same builder on Big Tancook Island, near Mahone Bay. That's near Lunenburg. The builder was a man named Mason whose family emigrated from France."

Harley explained. "The French who settled on Little and Big Tancook Islands had their names anglicized over time. That's how Masson became Mason and Langeville is now pronounced with an English twist. They grew potatoes and cabbages but also fished for a living. Some built their own schooners known for excellent speed and handling."

"Tancook schooners were called baby *Bluenoses* 'cause they had the same hull outline as the *Bluenose* and were just as fast," said William, remembering the librarian's information.

"Wicked fast," Harley confirmed.

Emmett handed William a dime. "The *Bluenose*. It's been on the back of the ten-cent piece since 1937. She raced and won for almost twenty years, long after her prime. Then she was sold to a company that used her to haul goods in the Caribbean. During the war, a U-boat captain surfaced and told the crew he couldn't live with himself for sinking the most famous racing schooner in the world. So he let her go. She broke her spine on a reef near Haiti in 1946." Emmett dispelled his sadness with a head shake.

"That won't happen to this beauty he bought when he wouldn't sail *Fathom*. The *Mary*." Emmett stroked the gunwale in a moment of reverence. William chimed in. "Mary, as in Granny?"

"Yup, Daniel named this beauty after the girl I … I introduced him to — who became your grandmother. When your father died, the wind went right out of Daniel's sails. He tried to put the *Mary* up for sale, so I bought her. To keep her in the family."

Harley added, "Trenton offered three times more, but Daniel sold her to Grandpa."

William squinted at the sun, thinking about what he was sailing back to. He hadn't been able to find gold or money in Saint-Pierre. Would his grandmother and mom agree to let him stay or would he have to go back and face Brad? Would his grandmother manage to get a private mortgage in Halifax or would they have to sell? Could he get Daniel to take *Fathom* out so somehow McCoy could show him what it was he had hidden for him? How did it go up and down? So many questions, so few answers. And then there was the race.

"Would Nathaniel have won if Granddad had raced last year?"

Emmett shook his head no. "Nathaniel was a fisher — a good navigator and a good man with a motor. But he could never harness the wind like Daniel."

"You think Nathaniel will race again this year?"

"He got ill after his win last year. His son Robert, the one you saw at the sail loft, took him in. He has a nurse and a guard there, round the clock in that big house."

"Then what were those sails he bought from you?"

"Robert bought his own sailboat," answered Harley.

"Why wouldn't he just sail his father's boat?"

"Nathaniel wouldn't let him. Cared little for him as a boy and less for him as a man. Nathaniel was obsessed with one thing: McCoy's gold."

"That family's had bad karma," said Harley with a wave of her hand that was meant to dispel the bad aura. William turned to Emmett for more details.

"Mother died in childbirth and the oldest son died in a freak fishing accident. Caught up in the nets. Nathaniel couldn't get his boy out in time."

"That's Thomas, the one who died about thirty years ago?" William remembered from the graveyard.

Emmett nodded, surprised he knew so much about it. "Was as if losing one son made it impossible for him to love the other — stupid, really. Robert left Lunenburg and went into real estate law in Toronto and Texas."

"Austin?" William asked, remembering the *Keep Austin Weird* bumper sticker.

"Yup. Apparently made a mint and came back last year when his father took ill."

Harley picked up the tale. "They say Nathaniel hasn't got long to live. I guess this is Robert's last chance to show his dad he's a sailor in his own right."

"You think Trenton can win?" William asked.

"With that boat, new sails, some luck, and Daniel not racing — good odds," said Emmett.

Harley waved William to come down to the galley and help her with a pot of soup on the stove. She had explained how the gimballed stove worked. It swayed back and forth on pivots that kept the stovetop level in side to side motion. Clever, he thought.

"Do you know what was in the Real McCoy's note that made Granddad so angry?"

"Nope. Years ago, before he left for Toronto, Jack had started to refit *Fathom*. Daniel was at a boat show and your father thought it would surprise him. Put in steel stays, winches, new knees, braces, tuned the engine. Boy, what an effort," sighed Emmett.

William and Harley waited to hear the outcome. Emmett scrunched his lips. "Daniel got angry. Said that boat belonged to a murderer and wasn't to come out and that was that. Jack had looked into the rumours concerning McCoy and Cavendish's death. He wanted to share his doubts. But Daniel's mind was made up and he wouldn't hear any of it. Daniel can be pig-headed. So Jack went to Toronto."

They were coming up onto the Funnel, and William thought he saw someone looking down at his grandfather's place. He took the binoculars hanging in the cockpit.

There, on a road bordering Daniel's land, stood Robert Trenton by his car with a set of his own binoculars. The lawyer made observations in a notebook. He then stole towards the boathouse, weathered a silvery grey by sun and salt.

He pulled on the rusty chain locking the doors but it wouldn't yield.

"There's Trenton now, Uncle Emmett. He's looking through a knothole in the wood to see *Fathom* in her cradle." He passed his binoculars to Emmett.

When they entered the Funnel proper William lost sight of the property for a few minutes. When it came back into view Trenton was nowhere to be seen. Emmett shrugged and readied the boat for mooring.

High tide made pulling the tender onto shore easier. William secured the painter to a tree. They followed the rutted road that circled up to Daniel's place.

"If the Real McCoy wanted to give Granddad a nice schooner like *Fathom*, why would he leave him a nasty note?" asked William, more to himself than anyone else. "And if he was a murderer why didn't the police charge him? Why didn't McCoy deny the accusations? None of it makes sense." Nobody argued.

They looked up to the empty rocking chair on the veranda, swaying in the breeze. Emmett cupped his hands and hollered, "Daniel? Daniel?" He listened for an answer before adding, "He might be having a nap inside. I'll check."

Emmett emerged shaking his head. "Must be out for a walk. Good sign."

Harley put an arm around William's shoulders as they stood on the veranda. "Nice work, William. We'll make a sailor out of you yet."

"You did good, too," he answered.

Emmett corrected him. "Well. You were good on the trip and you did well. Except for all that treasure stuff. Those rumours we could have thrown down an abandoned well."

Harley was about to scold Emmett when William put his hand up. "The well. Throw it down an abandoned well." He glanced over Daniel's property. His eyes lit upon something that made him stop short. "The well. The well. Holy cow!"

William sprinted past the tractor over to the well. "That's it! The Real McCoy said it would go 'up and down' and that it was 'hidden deep.' And at the Fisheries Museum, Manny said the rum-runners sometimes hid their stuff in unlikely places, like people's wells."

William pried the weather-beaten boards off the stone well. He peered into the black hole. There was a faint reflection off the water below. He dropped a small rock down the well … *clunk*. There was something there, other than water, not far below the surface. William and Harley turned to Emmett with a questioning look.

"Well, it's possible … people are still digging up stuff hidden during Prohibition."

The screen door clattered behind them as Harley, flashlight in hand, followed William, who dragged a rope and bosun's chair to the well. Emmett started up the little-used tractor. It signalled its displeasure with a belch of black smoke.

William slipped into the straps. Harley tethered the other end of the rope to the back of the tractor. He wasn't afraid of this water, but it was still a long way down.

Emmett ambled over and tugged on his rope. "Your gear will hold." With a flick of his wrist William snaked the rope questioningly towards the still running tractor. "My end will hold. That's a promise. But gear's only as good as the man operating it. Ready?"

William nodded and signalled to be lowered. What was down there?

Chapter Nineteen

Fathom

Fathom: a measure of six feet; also means to understand

Harley waved for Emmett to back up. The rope arching over the steel pulley creaked, and William thought he looked the part of a medieval witch-dunking.

Emmett's face was a mask of concentration as he inched William down. Harley directed the flashlight's beam as close to her cousin as she could. The light still spun crazily on the wall. William focused on a round wooden object beneath him. He secured the object with a bowline on a second line and double pumped to signal "up."

The tractor pulled him clear. William swapped his rope for the other. "Move her forward, Uncle Emmett!" The engine rumbled and strained as the mysterious wooden object was pulled steadily upward.

A barrel emerged into the sunlight, swinging from the steel pulley. William and Harley whooped their delight. Using William's rigging knife, Emmett scraped the dirt from the barrel's side. *Dark Rum* was painted in fading colours. When he shook the barrel and heard the sloshing inside William sighed. It wasn't gold.

They hammered the boards back on the well. William and

Harley rolled the barrel up to the shed and stood it up beside the weed whacker.

"Whatever the Real McCoy hid for Granddad," said William as they walked back to the veranda, "it's not in Saint-Pierre and it wasn't in that well."

"You still believe in the phantom's gold?"

"Yes! I can't prove it, but I'm sure it exists. And somehow Cavendish's death was involved. If Uncle Emmett's right, Granddad certainly won't just visit the boat. So we need to find a reason for him to sail *Fathom*, don't you think?"

Harley warmed to the idea. "Be kinda nice if Daniel sailed her in the race. If he gets his sea legs back he might get more work coming at the loft and …"

Emmett called out from the kitchen. "Louder and funnier, please."

"We were saying it would be good for Daniel to race *Fathom*," answered Harley.

"Well, of course it would. But it would take a lot to get Daniel to agree to sail her, let alone race her," mused Emmett. William and Harley waited for more of an explanation.

"First off, who knows what condition she's in."

"You tell us," challenged William, bolting for the footpath that led to the boathouse. Harley sprinted in his wake and that got Emmett to follow.

The right key and some oil allowed them to unlock and fling open the two seaside doors. The winch screeched the cradle down the rusty tracks into water that seemed to sparkle a greeting.

Emmett forgot to remove his shoes and roll up his pant legs. He ran his fingers along her hull one after the other. William thought he looked like he was playing a piano, which he accompanied by uttering an admiring, "My, oh my, oh my … Dogs and the devil, she's a beauty. You can see why Jack tried to restore her."

"I'm glad my dad didn't believe *Fathom* has a blood curse."

"Now the trick will be to convince Daniel." To nobody in particular he added, "You know, the name schooner comes from the Scottish 'to scoon,' or to skip a flat stone across the water. It was given to one of the first schooners launched in Gloucester, Massachusetts, in 1713. When Captain Robinson launched the first such vessel it was deemed to skip gracefully across the water. That's how the name schooner came to be. This one looks like she'd do a pretty skip, eh, Harley? Pity we don't have the means of stepping her masts."

Harley explained further, "A crane. We'd need to be in a boatyard or have a crane nearby to do that." Then she finished with the obvious, "We don't have a crane."

William smiled and pointed out to sea. "Captain Thornton does."

There was Thornton's Coast Guard cutter cruising up the coast.

Captain Thornton was enthusiastic. He said it would be good practice for his men to work on *Fathom*, to be better prepared for rescue efforts on older boats.

Like worker ants, his crew swarmed over the schooner. They pulled her rigging into place. They helped Emmett step her masts.

"William," said Emmett, "slip one of those boots over the end, will you?" He pointed to rubber cones with holes in them. William slipped the boots over the bottom end of the two masts before they were threaded through their respective holes in the deck.

Once below, Emmett lifted the boards that covered the keel and bilge and called up to the crew to lower, lower, lower the two masts that inched their way down. Now William understood Emmett's request not to pour bilge water down his back. The bilge was the area around the keel and beneath the floor boards. The water gathered there smelled of wet wood, wet paint, and diesel fuel. He might be imagining things but he also thought he detected the faint smell of fish — probably from its days as a fishing boat before McCoy bought it. Who would want that poured down their back? If it got too deep, Emmett explained, it got pumped out. William could feel the waves rocking the boat as they bubbled along her hull.

The mast had been sanded and varnished to a glossy smoothness that felt like a fine piece of furniture. William helped push the foot of the masts till each rested on its rightful step. It spread its weight over the keel. That minimized stress, Emmett explained. William could feel the extra weight settling the schooner deeper into the water. He held his breath. He was slipping deeper below the surface but then it stopped. Back on deck, he helped Emmett slide the boots down to deck level to keep water out.

The two Coast Guard mechanics nodded in appreciation at the way the diesel engine had been stored. They filled her tank with a few litres of fuel. She started up with the old hand crank. It didn't have a push button start, strictly old school. It reminded William of those old movies where they used a hand crank to start the cars. They all marvelled how little water seeped into her hull considering how long she'd been out of water. Could dampness and unfulfilled dreams have kept her seams tight? mused Emmett.

They motored away from the cutter and drifted towards their mooring, a big, orangey-red ball that floated above its anchor line. Harley passed William a long gaff hook. He stroked through the water until he hooked and pulled up the mooring line. They laid it through the hawse hole and over the bollard at the bow.

"Hawse hole" was the term Harley used. But the anchor rope didn't run through a hole. It was a two-foot-wide brass fitting, one on either side of the bow. It didn't quite close over at the top. It looked more like a set of brass bull horns curving in to each other but with enough of a gap to easily drop an anchor line.

The job Jack McCoy had started was finished. It had taken thirty skilled men from the Coast Guard just over four hours to pull her together. It had helped that his dad had all the parts she needed ready to go.

She bobbed at her mooring, within hailing distance of her twin, *Mary*. The two racehorses tugged impatiently at their bridles, aching to run with the wind, said Emmett.

The porch side door swung open. Daniel, windblown, in shorts and short sleeves, walked in. They jumped up and rushed him out to the veranda to see *Fathom*.

Emmett was the first to speak. "Now, before you get all riled up, the kids and I thought it might be a good idea to finish what Jack started here with *Fathom*. She's all set to sail, Daniel, if you would just ..."

"There is no way in hell I'm sailing that boat," snapped Daniel.

William piped up. "It was my idea, Granddad. I thought it would be a nice thing to do. You know, finish up my dad's project on the anniversary of his death."

That calmed Daniel right down but it didn't change his mind.

"That boat's got a blood curse on her. And who knows what condition she's in."

That stymied Emmett for a moment. "Then race my boat, your old boat. Sail *Mary*."

William was about to object. Sailing the *Mary* wouldn't get Daniel any closer to the Real McCoy, who only haunted *Fathom*. Harley came to his rescue.

"Actually, I hate to say it, but you can't lend Daniel your boat for the race. As chairman of the event, Grandpa, you must keep an arm's-length' relationship with the contestants. Those are the rules. I mean, I printed them out, remember?"

A pall descended over the room as Emmett took stock. "Well I guess that's that. There'll be no McCoys racing this year."

Chapter Twenty

The Raid

Cleat: a stationary object that allows a line to be secured on a vessel

William was brooding in *Fathom*'s cockpit, staring out at the tender that waited for him to admit defeat and row back to shore empty-handed. From the banquette he could see Harley watching him from shore. She finally pushed her bike back up the road.

The Big Dipper and the Little Dipper seemed so much brighter here. Certainly brighter than anything else in his life right now. It had been a long day. The gentle rocking of the boat was putting him to sleep.

William woke with McCoy slicing *Fathom* through dark water. "I don't know why you got me to sail to Saint-Pierre if we weren't going to find what you've hidden."

McCoy flashed a smile. "Learned to sail, though, didn't you?"

"I didn't come here to learn how to sail," he snapped. McCoy cranked in a line, heeling the boat further over.

William grabbed a cleat. "Look, I don't know how to get Granddad to sail *Fathom*. Nothing seems to work. And I've been waiting for you to tell me what you've hidden for a long time now ..."

"What would you know about a long time?"

"My dad's been dead for a year and it feels like ten —"

McCoy cut him off. "My soul's been lashed to this boat for sixty-two years" — he let out the jib — "and eight months" — he pulled in the main sheet — "two weeks, four days" — he pulled in the foresail — "twelve hours, eighteen minutes, eleven seconds … and counting."

Fathom was quiet except for the sound of her hull parting waves, gurgling like a child enjoying a playground while those around her argued.

"Listen, lad, what I've hidden is something Daniel needs."

"What about me?"

"You? You need to stop being angry at your dad for dying."

"I can take care of myself."

"By shredding your dad's sail and burying it?"

William jeered, "Oh, like you're one to talk. Look at the good job you've done with your family. Killing Cavendish really helped you get close to Daniel, didn't it? "

McCoy was dead, but his emotions weren't. "You're ruining my death here, boy. You know it takes two hands to hold onto a grudge — and two to sail a boat. So what do you want to do? Stay angry with your dad or learn to appreciate what he gave you?"

William blurted, "Appreciate? He left us. He was the one who —"

"Jack didn't have a choice. You do."

William crossed his arms.

"Life's gonna skin your shins on a good day without you running around shore rocks in the dark. And all you're left with in the end is sore shins and regret."

They sailed in silence. Then McCoy added, "You stay angry you'll end up like Trenton … or me." William stared ahead.

McCoy held his left arm aloft. “See that — those silhouetted gravestones sticking up like death’s picket fence?” William saw he was pointing at a coastal cemetery. “Better grab a tombstone ’fore the good ones are all taken. ’Cause a man who won’t help when he can or won’t take help when he needs it is as good as dead.”

William’s face was as stony as the gravestones.

“Right, time to fish or cut bait. Hang on.” A wave of his hand whipped the schooner forward. *Fathom* moved so fast she whistled. William grabbed a cleat with both hands.

Fathom slowed by a dock with a sign: *Trenton. Private. Trespassers will be prosecuted.*

McCoy lowered his voice. “I want you to sneak up there and bring me the hexagonal box from the old man’s bedroom — that’s a six-sided box. Do that and I’ll tell you what I’ve hidden for Daniel.”

William hesitated. Was this a setup? Was McCoy a murderer and not to be trusted? One thing was sure. He would only get his answer if he got McCoy what he wanted. He remembered what Manny had said about McCoy. He was called a straight man in a crooked world. More importantly, his father hadn’t believed he was a murderer either. His stomach still knotted when he stepped off and *Fathom* pulled away.

“When you get the box, come back here and I’ll pick you up. But be careful … he has a shotgun.”

William dropped to a crouch. He might have argued, but *Fathom* was out of sight.

He climbed towards the security lights bathing the sprawling house. Perspiration beaded on his forehead. His throat was dry.

In the distance, a big motorcycle driven at breakneck speed

splashed through a puddle. It slowed. Its headlight lit up the steel gate to the property.

The uniformed guard swung it open. The motorcycle pulled in and stopped. "Evening, George," said Robert Trenton. He draped his leather jacket over the backrest and his helmet on one of the mirrors. The engine *click, click, clicked* as it cooled.

Hugging the safety of the shadows, William inched closer. Trenton strode inside with the guard. Through the open door William saw the nurse jump to her feet. She flashed what his dad would have called a paid-for smile, a Brad smile. Her pen clattered to the floor. William snuck in through the door and hid behind a medical trolley. When George clumped back outside and the nurse bent down to retrieve her pen, William scurried up the stairs.

On the second floor he saw Trenton take a deep breath before entering an open door. William tiptoed into the room across the way. It was Trenton's home office and the trophy shrine. He read his grandfather's name on plaques across the base of the trophy.

He stared into the room across the hall. He saw Nathaniel Trenton, the emaciated patient with the oxygen mask. Trenton spoke to his father. "I wish I could take you out ..." His hand gesture implied "away from here," but he said, "sailing."

The patient pulled off his oxygen mask. "Never gonna get the gold or win the race with them soft lawyer hands. Go back to painting." His gaze turned back to the window. He sucked in oxygen through raspy lungs.

Eyes glistening, Trenton dropped back into the shadow of the hallway. He stared at his hands. "I don't know why you always treat me like ... like I'm from away. There isn't a moment goes by I don't wish Thomas had walked off the boat instead of me that day." There was no answer from his father.

As Trenton slunk off, William slipped into the room where

the old man lay with his back to him. He saw a schooner model with Trenton's yellow and gold pennant and the name *Mary* on its transom. He scanned the room for the six-sided box. He peered under the bed. He checked the armoire. It only contained a few clothes. Then he saw something on top of the armoire.

He climbed on a chair. It was the six-sided box. He opened it. Inside was a piece of brass equipment. He closed the top and latched it. *Nathaniel Trenton* had been carved into the oak top. He studied the brass straps. One had an embossed sun. The other side had an embossed crescent moon with a star at either end. This was the mark he'd seen in the police photos. This was what made the mark under Cavendish's cheekbone.

A hand grabbed his ankle. He screamed.

Nathaniel Trenton had rolled over and pulled his oxygen mask down. His eyes were feverish. "You find the gold yet, Jack?" Nathaniel's yellow teeth looked fiendish. He exhaled. His breath reeked of something long dead, something brushing his teeth wouldn't cure.

"What makes you so sure there is gold?"

"I seen it," he hissed. "Those gold bricks, I seen it." He knocked over a metal tray.

"You saw the gold because you were there, weren't you? You hit Cavendish with this box and left a mark on his cheekbone, didn't you? The mark was faint because it was done by you as a boy, not a big man like McCoy."

Nathaniel lay back on his pillows. He wheezed his reply. "If I hadn't stopped Cavendish from killing McCoy, I'd'a had my share. Nobody woulda said I was crazy to believe in it all these years. Mine. It shoulda been mine."

From the stairway a woman's voice called out. "Mr. Trenton, are you all right? I heard something fall. Why didn't you ring your buzzer, I would have come right —"

William sprang from the chair. Clutching the box, he whipped past the nurse towards the balcony.

"Hey! Who are you? What are you doing here?" She activated the intercom: "George, we have an intruder."

From the balcony, William could see the front of the house reflected in the garage windows. Trenton stood beside his motorcycle listening to George's walkie-talkie.

The nurse's voice carried in the night air. "Some kid just escaped out the south balcony. He's stolen a box from Mr. Trenton's room. I'm calling the police."

"How the hell did he get in?" growled Trenton.

"No idea, sir," mumbled George.

"Get the shotgun," ordered Trenton.

Chapter Twenty-one

The Escape

Davits: horizontal spars that allow a boat to be lowered over the side or stern

From his perch on the balcony, William stared down at the image of Trenton and George, the guard reflected in the garage windows.

George froze. "She said he was a kid, Mr. Trenton."

"She said he was a thief." Trenton yanked a double-barrelled shotgun from the hall closet. He checked both barrels then snapped the hinge with a murderous clack.

William studied the pines buffering the house against the sea. At one end was a brick wall. From the dock side Trenton and the guard hurried towards him.

William clamped the box's handle in his mouth. He leaped, plummeting between branches, tearing skin off his palms, scraping his elbow and bruising both thighs.

Trenton barked, "You go after him through the trees; I'll watch the dock."

William aimed to run along the dark seaside of the trees to the dock. Security lights stopped at the trees but here and there groped through the gaps to the rocks and sea.

George couldn't see him in the shadows. So he took a boxing

stance, his arms, like giant lobster claws, waiting to crunch the intruder when he emerged from the darkness. William's shoes were soaked from the dew and slipped on the grass. Police sirens wailed.

He sprinted at George with the box held out like an offering. At the last second he dove and slid between the guard's legs. He sprang to his knees and scooted back by the main lawn. The box banged against his leg.

George spun and fell. He called as he struggled to his feet, "He's coming your way!"

Trenton shielded his eyes, trying to see William's zigzagging form. Three feet away, William tossed the box over the fence and vaulted after it. He scooped up the box and ran.

George plowed into Trenton's back, sending them both sprawling through the gate. Trenton sat up and shot. *BOOM!* The fence finial beside William exploded.

BOOM. The second shot shattered the box apart, leaving only dangling brass straps. The piece of equipment clattered amongst the rocks.

Trenton threw the gun aside and pointed to the water. "Don't let him get away."

William stampeded down the dock screaming, "I'm here. Hey, where are you?"

Whoosh! Fathom cannonballed out of the darkness, parallel to the dock. Black smoke billowed from the half-barrel McCoy used to obliterate *Fathom*'s name from view.

"William, you'll have to jump if you want to make it."

William's eyes were wide with alarm. He wrestled with a choice between the water and his pursuers. At the very end of the dock, he leaped and landed on the deck with a thump.

McCoy exulted, "Ha, ha! Ha, ha! My God, that was great. Just like the old days!"

Through a gap in the smoke William saw Trenton punching

the air in a rage.

"Burning oil-soaked rags — that's an old rum runner's trick." George's admiring tone floated out to them. Then night wrapped the remnants of its disturbed quiet back around itself.

Lying flat on the deck, William panted as they rounded a rocky point.

McCoy laughed again. "Bullets, guts, and glory, my lad. Bullets, guts, and glory! Wasn't that fun? Wasn't it? Ha, ha. Yes, sir!" McCoy kicked the smoking barrel off the davits into the ocean and said, "Let's get you home." He gestured and the sails filled.

The schooner slowed as they came to Eastern Points. McCoy was still laughing. "That was just great. Haven't laughed like that since taking to the seas was a choice, not a sentence."

The adrenalin rush William got from his escape faded and he felt his scrapes and bruises. His teeth chattered as he spoke. "That was crazy. I mean putting me where I could be shot at for a stupid box?"

"It was a chance we had to take." He wrapped a blanket around William's shoulders.

"Yeah, well, next time you can take a chance with your own ass, okay?"

McCoy's grin surprised William. "My ass, as you so elegantly put it, knows what's in there. You needed to see it. You needed to know the enemy we're up against."

William rolled over on his back and took in the starlit night. "We?"

"We both want Daniel to sail, don't we?" He looked around. "You get the box?"

William held the brass handle and the strands of brass strapping but no box.

"I see. Nice try, lad. Nice try."

"What was in it? That instrument?"

"A sextant. An instrument to navigate by the sun and stars."

Why would McCoy need a sextant when he navigated so well without one?

"What happened that day, the day Cavendish was shot?"

"I fired Cavendish because of his drunken brawling. When he heard I was bringing back gold in 1947, he decided he'd highjack me. He knew I wouldn't bring it to Lunenburg but would use the little bay we knew from our rum-running days."

"How did he know what time you'd come through?"

"The bay is shallow and I was sitting low in the water because of the weight of the gold, so I had to pick the highest tide of the month. When I rounded the point at the narrow inlet, he was waiting. I was coming in quietly with little sail so I couldn't turn around and run for it. When I was about three feet from him he brought up his Webley revolver. Nathaniel was in it for robbery, not murder. I saw the lad hit Cavendish with that box just as the gun went off. The bullet didn't miss by much."

McCoy fingered the bullet's trajectory, past a chip in the main mast. "Cavendish was groggy but strong. He tried to take the revolver from Nathaniel, who'd picked it up. It went off, this time shooting Cavendish in the chest. The lad tried to stop the bleeding but it was too late. We heard neighbours coming. Nathaniel froze. I cleated a line to Cavendish's boat, leaned over, and grabbed him. He still held the pistol, so I made him drop it. As the sextant case had his name on it, I grabbed it too."

"How did he see the gold?"

"He was in shock, shaking violently. I opened the cockpit storage to find him a blanket, forgetting I'd hidden the gold bars there. So I gave him my coat and put him ashore. I was making for open water when I saw the coat slip off his shoulders."

"That coat with your initials was covered in blood. Why didn't the police arrest you?"

"Two policeman did come and see me — to ask about the coat and see if I wore a ring with a crescent moon, one that might have made the mark below Cavendish's cheek. The RCMP fellow was all for arresting and charging me. But the Lunenburg policeman — I think his name was Corkum — he was older, had been a sailor, and he said he'd seen a lot of fights. He didn't think I had hit Cavendish."

"Because you would have left a deeper imprint?"

McCoy nodded. "Cavendish and I were the same height. That Lunenburg policeman reasoned that if I were throwing a punch or hitting Cavendish with something in my hand we would have to be close, so probably on the same boat — his or mine. He showed the RCMP fellow that my punch would have come across and hit Cavendish on the cheek, not below it. He figured that whoever hit Cavendish in the face was shorter and smaller."

"Why didn't you tell the police it was an accident and that Nathaniel was involved?"

"Nathaniel saved my life. He was a thief, not a killer. Wasn't sure the police would make that distinction. Besides, one more rumour about me wouldn't make any difference."

"So why did you want me to get the case back?"

"I hoped that if you showed it to Daniel he'd believe I wasn't involved. That I didn't leave that mark on Cavendish's face or shoot him. Then he might sail *Fathom*."

William hugged the blanket. "Why does Nathaniel talk to his son like he hates him?"

"Nathaniel ignored Robert and obsessed about the gold. Now Robert wants to win his father's respect, and he thinks putting his name on the sailing cup is the way to do it. Now that his dad's dying, Trenton will do anything to win. You can bet your house on it."

Suddenly, the bow of the Coast Guard cutter appeared directly in front of them. William sat up. "There isn't any fog and we don't have a smokescreen to hide us."

"Nope, but that's Little Duck Island over there. Ready about. Helm's down."

This time William bobbed under the swinging boom. They headed away from the cutter, right for shore. Fear gripped William. He thought he'd be flung into the ocean.

McCoy pointed to a sixty-foot passage in the peninsula. "The Gut. We used it to outrun the Coast Guard in the old days — too shallow for them; they'd run aground. We've got to be careful of that, too — watch for mudbanks."

Fathom's moon shadow glided across one of the houses dotting the passage a mere twenty-five feet away. A second-storey light came on. The night was so quiet that they heard bedsprings creak, and a woman's voice carried over the water: "Vernon! Vernon, wake up. There's a sailboat coming through the Gut."

A man answered, "Holy old dynamiting Jesus, woman, go back to sleep. Only an idiot would risk a sailboat in the Gut." He paused before adding, "Or a right good sailor!"

William and the Real McCoy exchanged a smile. "That's the skill that Daniel has, the skill that Trenton will never have. You get your grandfather on this boat to race and I can give him what I've hidden for him."

"I tried, but Granddad won't sail *Fathom.* How am I supposed to ..."

"It might help if you tell him what I wrote on that note." McCoy leaned in and whispered the contents of the secret message.

William looked puzzled.

McCoy whispered it again. William's jaw dropped. "How could you write such a cruel thing to your son?"

"It wasn't cruel."

"Well, what else could it be?"

"There were treasure seekers — so I used code."

Chapter Twenty-two

The Wager

Mooring: a place or line that holds a vessel in place

William woke up in *Fathom*'s cockpit. He pulled the tender over, clambered in, and had rowed almost to shore when he realized he wasn't wearing his safety harness. He was too focused on persuading Daniel to race *Fathom.*

Daniel, his coffee cup in hand, stepped onto the veranda just as William ran up the hill towards him.

"Good morning, William. You're up and about early. Your dad was an early bird too."

William panted, trying to catch his breath. He stood beside his grandfather and pointed to *Fathom* tugging at her anchor chain. William said, "She's ready to go and you should be too. The Real McCoy didn't murder Cavendish."

Daniel choked on his coffee. "What do you mean he didn't murder Cavendish?"

He showed him the photo of Cavendish's face. "That mark was made by a smaller, shorter man than McCoy."

"So … you're saying McCoy had a shorter, smaller partner in this crime? Doesn't mean he wasn't involved," reasoned Daniel. He shook spilled coffee from his wrist.

William played his ace. "I know what the note said. The note McCoy left you."

Daniel shot him an incredulous look. "You couldn't possibly know ..."

"If I'm right, you have to promise to race Saturday."

"You're awfully ..."

"Hard-headed?"

"Pig-headed!"

"Runs in the family. Gimme your word on it?"

"You're wasting your time."

"Then you've got nothing to lose, Granddad."

Daniel weighed his options before heading in and back out before the screen door shut. He pried a yellowed note from behind a photograph of himself as a young man. He looked up, daring William to guess what only he and the dead man knew.

"Keelhaul!" said William.

Daniel turned the yellowed note to show William its inscription: *Keelhaul. Your father, William McCoy, 1947.*

"How did you know?"

"When you race on Saturday, you'll find out. And it wasn't meant to be a nasty note, you know."

"What else could it mean?"

"Race and you'll find out."

Harley and Emmett could hardly believe it when Daniel told them that he'd race. They pulled out charts, sat down, and pored over the race course.

Mary had called. She hadn't been able to secure a private mortgage. She was coming home today and then they would rethink what was to be done next.

A sports car rumbling to a stop outside drew Harley's attention.

"That's Trenton."

A moment later Trenton marched in. "Morning, everyone."

"Morning," answered Emmett as the others nodded a greeting in reply. Trenton's tie had a green sailboat on it that went with his green silk suit but not his cowboy boots.

Trenton looked to Daniel. "I saw that lovely schooner, *Fathom*, moored out in front of your place. Lot of work to get her in that shape. Were you planning on racing her?"

William, Harley, and Emmett turned to Daniel, who said, "Appears so."

Trenton made little knowing sounds. "I gather you're having trouble getting a mortgage … what with property values shrinking and you not working much in the sail loft these days." He slid two documents from his satchel onto the counter.

"My company is willing to buy your property at substantially above market value."

"Why would you want to buy my property?"

William jumped in. "So he can dig it up and find McCoy's gold for his father."

Daniel cleared his throat. "The property's not for sale, Mr. Trenton."

"Then consider a ten-year mortgage at generous terms. Time enough to get back on your feet." Trenton inched his mortgage certificate towards Daniel.

Daniel eyed it like a poisonous apple. "What's the catch?"

"We'd need to be sure you weren't taking any undue risks with your health."

Nobody seemed to know where he was heading with this line of thought. He continued. "For example, sailing in a race … could be dangerous. Too great a risk for my company to provide you with a mortgage."

Harley boiled over. "You'll provide a mortgage if Uncle Daniel doesn't race?"

"Call it protecting my company's investment."

"You're afraid to race against him," blurted Harley.

Trenton turned his palms upward in a gesture of mock resignation. "Think of it, Daniel. The bank calls your loan at the end of the month and you sell your house at a loss." He pushed the mortgage with the tip of his index finger. "Or you take my offer and you and your wife get to stay in the family house for at least another ten years."

Daniel reached out and pulled the document over to have a look at it.

"I bet Granddad can beat you," William boasted.

"That's very touching, but what would you bet?"

"The mortgage."

Trenton looked mystified.

"If Granddad wins, you give him the same deal that's on the table now."

Trenton hooted a dismissive laugh as he headed for the door.

William spoke up. "Didn't you want to prove to your father that you can beat a McCoy? Isn't that why your painting shows your boat beating the *Mary*?"

Trenton's eyes narrowed and he lurched towards William. Emmett stood by William.

"And if I win?" growled Trenton, stopping in his tracks.

William knew there was only one other thing Trenton wanted for his father. "You get the *Mary*."

Harley gasped.

Trenton took stock. "She's a pretty boat, but not worth the value of the mortgage."

"She is to your father. Do we have a bet?" asked William, standing his ground.

"You in a position to make that bet?" queried Trenton, glancing at Daniel and Emmett.

William looked up to Emmett, who, as owner, was the only one who could take the bet. Emmett placed a hand on William's shoulder to show that he backed the wager.

Daniel protested. "Emmett! You can't."

Emmett locked eyes with Trenton. "Just did. Deal?"

Trenton asked, "Daniel races *Fathom*, and if I win, I get the *Mary*? If Daniel wins, he gets the mortgage?"

Emmett nodded. Trenton spat, "Deal."

Emmett clarified the terms. "And Dingle acts as broker, so everything's fair."

Trenton kept his best shot for the end: "Tell me, Daniel, where are you going to get a suit of sails for *Fathom*? I mean, you aren't seriously going to race with those heavy, worn, cotton sails on her now, are you? Those rags'll tear at the first gust of wind."

Daniel frowned, so Emmett spoke up. "Well, ah, Daniel was asking to borrow mine."

Trenton pulled the rule book from his back pocket and held it like a preacher holding up a bible. "And you, as race chairman, were about to tell him the rules prohibit you from being personally involved with any of the contestants, right? Of course, Daniel could buy them — at market value. But you can't lend him the money." The room went deathly quiet.

"Let me know what you want to do, Daniel. You take my mortgage offer and don't race, or you find some sails and race for your mortgage." Trenton strutted for the door.

The sound of his sports car ebbing in the distance let the tension out of the room.

Emmett patted William's shoulder. "You've got the nerve of a highliner, there, lad."

William saw Daniel weighed down by the stakes. "He has more money than us but he doesn't have your sailing skills, Granddad." That was a hard one for Daniel to argue. William added, "Yesterday we didn't have a captain. Today all we don't have is a set of sails. And we have four days till the race."

Harley warmed to the idea. "Riiight! I could call and email some of the other sailing clubs and ask about sails. Wicked idea, William." She skipped to the computer.

Emmett managed a faint grin at the two cousins. "Genius is also born of enthusiasm."

William had just filled and plugged in the kettle when Harley called out by the computer. "Hey, guess what? Charlie Kaulbach at the Chester Yacht Club already wrote back and says he has a set of sails that would fit and they only want fifteen hundred dollars for them. Wicked, huh?"

"Fifteen hundred dollars? Might as well be a million. And the house, Mary's home ...," muttered Daniel. They all grew quiet and left Daniel to weigh his choices.

Chapter Twenty-three

Apple Crisp

Heeling: the angle a ship leans under pressure from the wind

As the big rocks to his granddad's laneway came into view, the breeze died down as if winded from following William's bike so closely. The seas were still high. The breakers rolled in over the sand bar. White foam ran up the shore like a loom trying to weave water to sand.

Cinnamon fragrance wafted into the yard. Apple crisp was cooking. Harley was right; his granny was home. He threw his right leg over the rear wheel and glided, standing on the left pedal. Jumping off the bike at the stairs, he let momentum careen the bike forward until it flopped on the grass. Its rear wheel whirred a dying protest. He leaped the two porch stairs and rushed into the kitchen. He found his grandmother cleaning dishes in the sink.

She spun as he creaked the screen door open and hardly had time to wipe her wet hands on her apron. He gave her a big hug. "Oh, Willy-boy!"

"When did you get back, Granny?"

"Harley's mother dropped me off. You must have passed her on the highway. I was just telling your mother that I hadn't had much chance to spend time with you."

He tensed up.

"I gather you and your mother are having a difference of opinion."

"She's got a new boyfriend and she wants to sell the house," he exclaimed, certain she would side with him.

"I see." His granny kept her voice neutral.

"She says he's just a friend from work but he's, like, always around. It bugs me. Especially when he tries to be nice to me."

"I can see how somebody being nice to you can be annoying," she said.

"He just pretends to be nice. He's a fake. And the house? Isn't it my house too?"

"Maybe your mother doesn't know what she feels."

The oven timer bell dinged. With heat-scarred oven mitts, Granny transferred the apple crisp to a trivet. She cut and slid two squares onto plates, dropped a scoop of ice cream on each, then handed him the biggest piece and a fork.

"Do you remember your Dad used to say the ice cream looked like a white octopus stretching across the apple crisp?" They watched the vanilla tentacles slither through the cracks in the baked brown sugar and laughed at the memory.

They ate a few bites before she returned to their original topic. "There isn't a widow's handbook to tell your mother how to deal with all this ..." She circled her hands, tossing in the complications surrounding his father's death.

"Boy, this is good. I was dreaming about your apple crisp."

"I'm glad you like it. I think you're having a good influence on your grandfather." William managed a smile. "I think you came here to try to find life as it was before your father's death. I know it isn't the same, but we both love having you here." He realized her shoulders were frailer than the look in her eyes tried to project.

He put his plate down and gave her a hug. He kissed her cheek, wishing it was a magic kiss that would soften her world, wishing it could bring his mother here, bring his father back, and wishing his world different than it was.

"Why does Granddad say Mom is responsible for Dad's death?" He took another bite.

She gave a little shrug. "They called your granddad the Rock because he gave everybody shelter or something to anchor to. Everybody but himself, in a way."

She stopped to eat some apple crisp and to gather her thoughts. "He was a bit distant with your father — loved him, but from a distance. Your grandfather put much stock in safety, providing a secure home. In the process, well, he lost sight of the fact Jack needed to be his own man. Daniel hadn't had a father to show him how to do it properly."

"Did Granddad have a bad childhood?"

"No, he just had a famous father who wasn't around. His mother was a strong woman from a strong family. That's what it took to bring up a son when you weren't married back then."

She washed their plates before continuing. "When your mother and father decided to move to Toronto, Daniel was keen to invest in your father's sail loft. His way of keeping his son close. Then Jack died, so unexpectedly like. Well, I think he was desperate for an explanation for the horrible accident, so he blamed her. When somebody dies we often wonder if there wasn't something we could have done to save them. That guilt can wear at you if you let it. You don't always think clearly. In time it becomes more about the pointing than about the point and harder to accept that it was nobody's fault. That darn stupid luck killed your dad. Everybody deals with their anger and sorrow differently."

William stared to see if she was talking about him and how

he felt about his dad. "You seem to have coped with it better than Granddad."

"Did you get angry with your dad when he died?"

He nodded.

"I did too." She looked out to the ocean. "Angry thoughts are like pieces of an ice floe that promise rescue. But they just break off and plunge you deeper into the cold waters of despair. Daniel blamed your mother, then got depressed. I cried a river of tears, then got angry with Jack. I mean, how could someone with such a good heart have such a bad one? I used to think that Jack should have done something to take better care of himself."

"Me too. How'd you stop thinking that?"

Mary opened the pantry door and pulled out a book. It had a worn leather cover. She opened it at a page marked with a dried rhododendron bloom. "Here, read this."

It was his father's handwriting. "Mom and the Rock held a BBQ for the family and I finally got to meet baby Harley. When Dad took Harley's parents sailing, she ran down the hill crying, waving her little arms. Ferne called Harley, who turned around, took her hand, and walked back up to the veranda. She's the mother I want for my children."

"Doesn't sound like the observations of an uncaring man, does it?"

He shook his head no.

"Whenever I get depressed about his death, I read a passage. I get to know what he was thinking. In a small way I feel like he's talking to me." Here she put her palms to her eyes and shook away a tear. "Was your father right about Ferne being a good mother?"

He shook his head yes.

"Sometimes life seems long, sometimes short. But we're only passing through, so dwelling on anger is just a waste of good time.

Love of another is not an easy thing to find, to cultivate and grow. But it's the best thing this life offers." She hugged William.

Two pieces of paper fell from the book. One was a photograph of Trenton digging by the boathouse with the hexagonal box beside him. The other was the photo of Cavendish's face with the markings. So Emmett was right, his father had tried to prove to Daniel that McCoy wasn't a killer.

"You, ah, you think Granddad will be okay?"

"It's a storm that had to run its course."

Then she looked back out to the Atlantic. "I wish he'd take to the sea again. There's nothing like a big ocean to help him get his bearings." Her face got sorrowful.

They both stopped talking for a moment. The house was filled with the sound of the ticking clock, the tinkle of wind chimes, and the distant surf rubbing against the shore. It sounded like the soft snores of a man sinking into a peaceful sleep.

"I think he's going to take Mr. Trenton's offer to provide a mortgage," said William.

"Trenton? His company turned us down for a mortgage."

"Mr. Trenton came by the sail loft, offered Granddad a mortgage ... if he doesn't race on Saturday. I think Granddad's going to take the offer."

His grandmother squared her shoulders, walked to the phone, and dialled. "Daniel, what's this I hear you're thinking of not racing?" She listened to his grandfather's explanation then cut him off. "I will not be your jailer, Daniel. If you don't race you'll be thinking of that race till it kills you, and it will kill you in short order. Please don't interrupt me, Daniel. I'd prefer to live in reduced physical circumstances than reduced spiritual ones. I'll be hungry and poor before I'll be a widow."

William heard his grandfather start to say something. She cut off his explanation. "I will not see you trade the security of this place at the cost of your soul."

William marvelled at her strong, steady tone, not bullying, just sure of itself. She finished with, "Then I suggest you find a way to get those sails. I won't keep you from that task any longer. Goodbye, Daniel." She placed the phone back in its cradle and gave William a nod as if to say, "That's that, then."

"I pushed Jack to leave," she confessed to him. "I knew he looked up to his father so much he'd put his own happiness on hold to stay with him. I told him to strike out on his own and to come back as his own man. It's time Daniel forgave the sea what she took from him and remembered what she gave him."

Her earlier frailness was gone. Maybe that's what you needed in times of trouble: to be more worried about someone else, someone else's cause.

"We just have to find a way to get money for sails," he said, summing up their predicament.

That made his granny smile. "Your father always scrounged stuff he'd find on the beach. He stored it in the shed, and when he wanted something badly enough, he'd find somebody to sell it to. That's how he was able to buy that dinghy that's in the shed."

The shed. A light went off in his head. He knew where to get money.

Chapter Twenty-four

The Devil to Pay

Ready about: a call to indicate a change of course or tack

Emmett snuck his SUV up to the Taffrail Pub's service entrance. William knocked softly at the door. He scanned the lane to be sure they were alone. Manny stepped out.

With the use of a dolly they wrestled the barrel of rum they'd pulled from the well onto a basement cradle. Manny tapped a spigot into the bung hole. He poured a large measure into a cup and sipped it.

He beamed. "Anybody don't like that, don't like black-eyed peas."

Emmett smiled in anticipation and said, "We've got the lad to thank for that." Manny shook William's hand and in the process bobbed the cup up and down in his left hand.

Emmett tried to grab it before he sloshed all of the precious amber liquid onto the floor. "Hang on there, Manny; you're spilling the peas all over the place."

Manny steadied the cup and started to offer it to Emmett but swung it in front of William, saying, "Maybe the lad would like a pea?"

William shook his head. "Oh, no thanks, I had a pee before we left."

Emmett and Manny doubled up with laughter. Manny shook so hard he fell to the floor, trying unsuccessfully to avoid spilling the rum.

Emmett hiccupped a laugh. "I'll be sure to eat every carrot and pea on my plate."

The two men howled until they cried, and that got William into the laughter too, although he wasn't quite sure what they were laughing about. It was just good to laugh.

Half an hour later Emmett and William drove back to D & E Sailmakers. William flicked the crisp hundred-dollar bills Manny had paid them. The barrel held almost thirty gallons, or more than one hundred litres, of well-aged rum. Manny said he knew more than a few customers who would love to sip a dram of bootlegged rum.

Emmett had told Manny to pay the thousand dollars to William for finding the rum. That's how he came to counting the bills over and over again. They drove past the Now & Then Antique store with its captivating display, pulled up to the sail loft, and parked.

"Dogs and the devil take us if we fail to get him his sails, eh, William?"

"There'll be the devil to pay," he shot back.

"What would we be worth to the devil anyway?" Emmett replied. That's when the second light came on in William's head.

"What *would* you pay for the devil?" he muttered, looking towards the antique shop.

"What's that?" asked Emmett, his foot on the bottom step to the loft.

"I'll be back in a bit, Uncle Emmett." He shot his bike down the road.

William slowed to study the ceramic clock with the devil's face in the antique store's window before pedalling standing up to pick up speed.

He wove his bike past the ornate turn-of-the-century bandstand. The same ponytailed musician sang a fast-paced tune that pushed his legs up and down like pistons.

William pounded his bike off the highway and up his grandparents' lane. Perspiration soaked his T-shirt as he ran into the house. He yelled "hi" and "goodbye" to his startled grandmother. He secured a cardboard box to the rear carrier with bungee cords.

William shot back along the highway to Lunenburg. The breeze rustled shoreline bushes. It sounded to William like applause for his plan.

Harry Pearce was astonished to see William panting with the box in hand. "I've come to talk to you about the devil." William laughed as he dripped with perspiration.

"Come in and have a cup of tea," said Pearce, his voice tinged with concern. He motioned for William to sit down while he fussed with a teapot and a box of biscuits.

William handed him the box he had carried back from his grandfather's place. Pearce opened it and admired the contents. He removed the newspaper wrapping and put the devil-faced bowl and pitcher that William had retrieved from the tunnel on the counter. He whistled appreciatively to see they matched the ceramic clock in his window.

From the kitchen, the teapot added its whistle of approval.

When they had finished their tea and William had wolfed a few biscuits, Harry Pearce took out a pad and scribbled some numbers on it to show William his offer.

William jerked his thumb to the harbour. "That won't get Granddad the sails."

"How much more, then?" Mr. Pearce pursed his lips as if the idea of more money left a bitter taste.

"Two hundred more."

Pearce sighed as he calculated his dwindling profit. Trying to look resolute, William shoved his hands in his pockets and felt a little packet he had forgotten about.

"You're asking a lot there, son. Be eating up my profit on this sale."

William put Brad's bracelet on the counter. "This diamond bracelet's been in the family for … well, too long now, and we don't need it. How much would that be worth?"

Pearce studied the bracelet with a jeweller's eyepiece. "Who told you these were diamonds? Because they're not. They're pretty enough, but these are zirconium, not really worth much at all. And it's been artificially aged."

William's laughter as he slapped the counter caught Pearce by surprise.

"It's a fake! Of course it is. That's too funny. Uh, Mr. Pearce, could I ask you to do me a favour? Send an email to my mother, Ferne McCoy, and tell her exactly what you told me about the bracelet?" He scribbled her email address on a piece of paper.

"Ah, yes, I can do that."

"Thanks." William placed his rigging knife on the counter. "How about this? It's mine. It was the Real McCoy's, then my father's. And now it's mine to sell."

Pearce put a hand out to the knife, paused, then nudged it back. He bought and sold bits of the past. But the knife was part of maritime history and belonged in the boy's present and future. So he pulled his wallet out, peeled off five hundred-dollar bills, and shook on the deal.

Chapter Twenty-five

The Calm Before the Storm

Bosun's chair: a planked or strapped seat
to hoist a sailor working on rigging

Emmett and Harley hurried over as William laid the hundred-dollar bills on the counter. "The devil paid me," he said with a laugh. "Now we can get Granddad's sails!"

Harley counted the money out then counted it a second time, her voice rising till she got to fifteen hundred dollars. She let out a whoop and gave William a bear hug.

"I don't know how you did it, Toronto boy, but as far as I'm concerned, you're not from away."

Emmett came over and draped an arm around them both. William thought he saw Emmett brush away a tear before heading over to the upstairs loft to tell Daniel the good news. Harley let her hand rest on William's shoulder as they listened to the murmured conversation. There was a brief silence before Emmett skipped back down the stairs and gave them both a wink.

Emmett and Harley left to deliver the spinnaker sail they'd repaired for Mr. Dingle. Daniel came out of the sail loft. He could tell his grandfather was feeling awkward.

"Look, Harley will be my first mate for the race. But she'd like you to crew with us." Daniel looked at his grandson with affection and pride. "I'd like you to crew with us too." William was speechless. Daniel mistook his silence as doubt about his offer, so he repeated himself. "I really would like you with me."

"Of course I'll be there with you, Granddad." He just hoped he'd be up to the task.

The next day William, Daniel, Emmett, and Harley hoisted *Fathom*'s new sails.

"Know what?" asked Harley as she was being lowered on the bosun's chair. William shook his head no. "Your dad made these sails."

William frowned his disbelief. "They've got the D & E Sailmakers logo on them."

"Yeah, but what colour is your dad's logo?" she persisted.

"Blue and red."

"See that extra stitching at the clew?" She was pointing to the lower portion of the sail closest to the mast. He looked closely and saw the blue and red overstitching. "That was your dad's signature touch during his last year at D & E. Before he headed out to Toronto and opened his own sail loft. Cool, huh?"

"Really cool." William touched his father's stitching. It might bring him good luck. There'd be four generations of McCoys in this race.

"Oh, I almost forgot." Harley yanked a printed copy of an email from her back pocket. "This came for you this morning."

It was an email with his mother's company logo, addressed to all staff: "Please be informed that Brad Goodwin has chosen to leave our employ." His mother had added a note for him. "Thanks for catching the fake, Willy-boy. After the email you had

Mr. Pearce send about the bracelet, I wondered what else Brad had lied about. Turns out he never attended Harvard University. And he isn't the B. Goodwin who wrote the article on wind and tides like he claimed on his work application."

There was another page, this one with a photo of their home. It took him a moment to realize that the for-sale sign had been uprooted and laid against the wall. His mother had scribbled a note here too. "Sometimes being a parent means listening to your children before making decisions. Your father and I bought this house, but you saved our home. It will be here for you when you want to come home. Brad won't be. You remind me more and more of your father — striving for things others would wilt from. Keep his memory close, Will. That way you'll keep him close to me too. Your father would be proud that you're racing with your granddad. I wish you both well with the race. Much love, Mom."

Harley gave him a hug. He had saved his home. Would they be able to save his grandparents' home?

Mid-morning, Daniel took his crew for a test run through the Funnel made by the island and the sand bar. They came abreast of it. William realized that in fact it was made up of two segments that parted in the middle right where the island bulged inward. Harley told him they called that "the saucer" because of its round shape.

Harley delighted in finding a lead depth finder from days gone by. It had been left in one of *Fathom*'s lockers, but with a newer line. She showed him how to sling lead, tossing it forward and counting the depth marked in fathoms on the rope.

"Mark one, mark twain, mark three, mark four … and a half, or thereabouts. A fathom being six feet, that's about twenty-seven feet of water beneath us."

"Mark Twain?" asked William.

"Yeah, that was the way they called 'two' out in the old days. That's where the writer got his name; he was born Samuel Clemens, but he went by the pen name Mark Twain."

The GPS in the Blackberry phone Paul Dingle had lent them showed their exact location in the Funnel. It chirped. William jerked the phone up but caught it before Harley had finished laughing. "William, it's Emmett. Tell that grandfather of yours *Fathom* makes a fine figure. We'll see you for dinner. Bye."

They left the Blackberry on the chart table in the cabin for tomorrow's race. The fuel gauge showed a few gallons of diesel, courtesy of the Coast Guard. That would get them to the race if they needed their motor. William got quite used to running about with his harness tied to the lifeline.

They made it to the open ocean through the Funnel. They tacked over and over, hoisted a sail, lowered a sail, and got the feel for her, which wasn't very difficult because she was the *Mary*'s twin.

Harley stretched out like a cat in the sun. She closed her eyes while they stayed on that tack. They put the boat through a number of drills until well into the afternoon. The wind dropped to almost nothing. It was saving itself for tomorrow's race.

William used tongs to pluck pieces of chicken from the barbecue to the dinner platter. He saw a Cape Islander coming around the point. He didn't recognize her colours as one of the local boats. The sun glared off its windshield. Impossible to see inside. He placed the barbecued vegetables beside the chicken and noticed the Cape Islander had dropped anchor about two hundred metres from *Fathom.* He also thought he saw a flipper break the surface of the water a couple of times quite close to *Fathom.* Maybe a turtle or a seal, he thought. He rang the old school bell. Dinner was served.

For the first time since his arrival everyone gathered for dinner around the picnic table by the side of the house. Harley and Emmett were going to spend the night at Daniel's place so they could get an early start.

In the midst of passing around bread, butter, coleslaw, baked potatoes, broccoli, and chicken, they all looked at a photo album. Emmett held it up so all could see a group of young men. One held a sailing cup in one hand and a bucket on a rope in the other.

His grandfather smiled, recollecting the moment that photo had been taken. "I did get him, didn't I? Red right rudder rule."

That prompted a gale of laughter from Emmett and Daniel. William and Harley smiled in polite anticipation of an explanation. Emmett was only too happy to give one between bites of chicken and swallows of iced tea.

"Paul Dingle thought he could win the race by tying a bucket to Daniel's keel."

William shook his head to show that he wasn't following the logic of the story.

"They call it a sea anchor or a drogue. You drag it to slow your forward progress in a storm. Of course tying it to another racer's boat is cheating," said Emmett.

Emmett waved a drumstick in the air like a conductor trying to bring his unruly orchestra back to order. "So anyway, at the very next race, Dingle has the right of way and Daniel should be the one to veer off, but that would cost Daniel precious time at the starting line. So he yells, 'Red right rudder rule.'" Emmett had to pause to catch his breath.

"Now although he has the right of way, Dingle doesn't know it and thinks the rules dictate he give way. He drops his helm so sharply he falls forward, catches his foot on a sheet, stumbles to the hatchway cover that slides so fast he's catapulted over the stanchion where he hangs staring at the masthead."

Mary and Harley joined the laughter that had them wiping tears from their eyes. William finished chewing a mouthful of coleslaw. "Which means what, exactly?"

Daniel took a sip of his iced tea. "Well, 'red right rudder rule' simply doesn't exist. But Dingle thought it meant I had the right of way, so he turned his boat away from the starting line, caught his foot on the mainsail sheet, and tried to steady himself on the hatchway cover. But it slid forward under his momentum, sending him flying over the railing, hanging by his ankle and staring at the top of the mast."

"The story's not as funny in English, is it?" observed William, whose attention was drawn to a splash that seemed to come from *Fathom.* He caught sight of what he thought was a flipper. He didn't know you found seals could be found this close to shore.

Chapter Twenty-six

The Trap

Drogue: a conical sea anchor used to slow a boat down in a storm

It was dark the next morning when William sat and fingered the model sailing dinghy's hull, from stern to bow, appreciating her fine lines. No thought of hurling it from the window crossed his mind now. He could hear Harley and his grandmother's nervous chatter in the kitchen. It smelled of pancakes and coffee. It reminded him of his father. It smelled good. After he died, Ferne took to buying her coffee on the way to work. He looked forward to the idea of making coffee for his mother like he'd done for his granddad.

At the door jamb he measured his height and recorded it in pencil as "William, 13 years." It was still a couple of inches higher than his dad's at the same age.

Racing with Daniel was something Jack did when he lived in Lunenburg. Last year would have been their first time together in years. Now, a year after his father's death, William was going to race with his grandfather. Was he up to the task?

He stood with his hands on the two marks on either side of the door, hoping for inspiration before taking his place as a member of *Fathom*'s crew.

He stopped at his grandfather's bedroom. Daniel pulled on a

warm sweater. Emmett sauntered in, carrying a box of new deck shoes. "I got you these."

Daniel raised an eyebrow. "You didn't have to …"

Emmett took the whistle from the bureau and handed it to Daniel. He slipped the lanyard around Daniel's neck, then reached under his sweater to tuck it into his chest pocket. Emmett took a rigging knife from the bureau, tied it to Daniel's belt, and then dropped it into the leg pocket of his cargo pants. He handed Daniel his compass. Daniel held it out to the window pointing through the Funnel. He nodded, satisfied that her bearings were true, and slipped it into his other leg pocket. He looked to William like an old gunfighter gearing up for one last, big showdown. He felt proud to be there with him.

They hurried through breakfast before gathering for a moment on the veranda. The ocean was reasonably flat. The wind chimes tinkled the wind's faint enthusiasm for a race. The moon showed wisps of fog lying around, mostly by the island. It looked to William like an Egyptian mummy had snagged strips of its bandages to the island's nearside rock face and across the Funnel. From the middle of the island, pines jutted high through the fog like jousting lances warning they'd impale anyone who approached.

It could have been intimidating. But he was with his granddad, the Rock, in his checkered shirt, calm and ready. "Right. Time we were off," he said patting his granny's shoulder.

They rowed out in silence. Once aboard *Fathom,* William cranked the engine to life. It *thrub*, *thrub*, *thrubbed* its presence through the darkness. The pump coughed cooling water out the back in spurts as if the smell of diesel smoke made the boat sick.

Wearing his safety jacket, he helped Harley hoist the jumbo- and foresails that chattered their impatience to move forward in the light winds. They dropped their mooring line through the hawse hole. He secured the tender to it for their return. They headed forward, the engine in readiness should the wind fail them in strength or direction.

They were in the Funnel. The engine missed, caught, missed again, then caught and carried them a few hundred metres in before dying altogether.

A man's concerned voice, probably Emmett's, called but failed to reach them clearly.

Daniel tapped the fuel gauge. It continued to read empty. That made no sense. Daniel looked at the compass setting and tethered the wheel spokes on course. He raised the engine's cowling and wrinkled his nose at the smell of diesel fouling his bilges.

"There's a leak. There's … somebody left the bleeding valve open. We're out of fuel." His tone was stark but without panic. He dropped the cowling back and looked forward. He slipped the restraints off the helm and took her under his control. He glanced down at the compass in the binnacle and steered by its reckoning.

The island and the sand bank wafted in and out of view as the fog did its best to knit a shroud around them. What moonlight made it through the fog gave the boat soft lines.

"William, head up to the bowsprit and keep an eye, will you?" It was a question that brooked no argument. "Harley, go down and bring me the GPS." He added "please."

Harley sprang from the hatchway. "Somebody took the battery. We have no GPS, no cellphone."

"Probably whoever drained the diesel into the bilges. Possibly someone who didn't want to lose a bet," reasoned Daniel.

William glanced back from the bowsprit but forced himself to stay as instructed. Daniel waved Harley to the helm. He stepped up on deck, steadying a hand along the boom.

The ocean squeezed by the Funnel was more tempestuous than by the shore. It sloshed over the freeboard onto the deck. They heard the insistent clanging of the school bell from the veranda. It implied a warning. But what? Emmett was alarmed by something the crew couldn't see in the low-lying fog.

William toed the wet grit. "Hey, Granddad, there's sand washing over the deck."

Daniel skimmed his hand over the water running by the coaming and felt the sand for himself. "Port your helm, we're too close to the sand bank," he called back to Harley, who threw the wheel to port. The bell stopped its warning.

His granddad hustled back to the cockpit. He compared his hand-held compass to the one on the binnacle. "Straighten her out and resume your previous course, here." He tomahawked the air with his hand to show Harley her new course. He unclipped the small compass and gave it to her for reference. They checked port and starboard for any glimpse that they were too close to rock or sand.

Fathom was now well into the Funnel. "William, come back here." When he hustled back to the cockpit Daniel summarized their predicament. "The fog's scheduled to burn or blow off in a bit. I was counting on the motor, the GPS, and the compass to get us through. But someone doesn't want that to happen." Daniel opened the banquette and wordlessly handed Harley a life jacket and shouldered one himself. A chill deeper than the one carried by the fog descended on the boat. They were at risk, and one didn't tow a tender in a race.

He put his big hand on William's shoulder. He lowered his voice so it sounded personal but irrefutable. "I don't want to alarm you, but if we hit a rock we may have to jump for it and swim for the island. Your safety rope could tie you to *Fathom* so tightly you won't be able to undo the bowline. I can't sail her if I have to worry about you too. I need a man I can count on to handle himself."

"I'm your man, Granddad." The big hand gave his shoulder a gentle squeeze. William undid his hook from the safety line and coiled it onto one of the mast's belaying pins.

"We'll turn back, sail around the island. I'll take the helm. Harley, I want you up in the bosun's chair to tell us when we're in the Bowl. That's the widest part of the Funnel and we can come about." He secured the wheel's spokes to lock her on course.

Harley looked stunned. "We don't have enough leeway to turn her safely. We could side-slide onto the island's rocks, we could —"

"I know," Daniel said matter-of-factly as he pulled the bosun's chair from the locker along with the lead and measuring rope they'd used the day before. "It's low-lying fog so you should be able to see better from up there."

They cranked her up. She called down, "This is good. I can pretty well make out the island and the sand bank. The edge of the Bowl is about three hundred metres ahead … we're pretty much dead in the middle." She tsked at her unfortunate choice of words.

The light winds, checked by the island, blew softly abeam from the port side. With only two small sails up, the boat didn't race forward or heel far over. They'd be a few minutes before they got to the Bowl. Daniel handed William the sounding lead and rope and tapped his shoulder to follow him forward.

"Sound away," he directed. William swung the lead the way Harley had shown him and counted out the depth. Three times he took measurements from twenty-four to thirty feet of depth. Daniel looped his index finger in the air for William to coil the rope.

Daniel pulled a measured amount of anchor rope that ran longer than the deepest sounding. He secured it to the bollard behind the bowsprit while he got William to tie the other end to the spade anchor with a bowline knot.

"Can you throw this over the side when I tell you? A good few feet out so as not to scrape the hull?" William spread his feet, bent his knees, and hefted the brutish steel with a grunt. That Daniel was worried about scratching the hull was reassuring.

"You have your rigging knife?"

William patted the lanyard from his belt loop to hip pocket.

"We're almost there, maybe fifty metres," called Harley.

Daniel scrambled back to the cockpit and lowered Harley. They scuttled to where William knelt at the bow.

"Okay, we're going to club haul her. When I tell you to, toss the anchor over the lee side. I'll wait till the wind spills out of her. When she catches it'll bring her head 'round right quick without slippage. As soon as she catches and spins I'll yell 'cut her' and you use your knife right here."

Daniel drew his index finger across the strands of anchor rope, six inches from where she was knotted to the bollard. "This is the only way to bring her around in such a narrow body of water without ripping the bottom out of her. Don't pull your knife out or open the blade till you've tossed the anchor. We don't need any accidents right now."

Nervousness bubbled a laugh out of William. Was there a good time to cut yourself with a knife?

William studied the anchor and rope. Could it spin the tons of sailing schooner and her momentum around safely? Harley's expression spelled doubt.

"It's very old school, hard on the rigging, but under the circumstances ..." Daniel left the thought unfinished and clambered back to the cockpit. Harley jumped after him.

The wind picked up and lifted the ribbons of fog to show they were right in the middle.

"Ready about, helm's down," Daniel called out in a voice strong and sure to reach his crew. Just as the wind eddied out of the sails he ordered, "Drop anchor."

William used his thigh muscles to propel the heavy chunk of anchor a few feet out. It hit with a splash that sprayed his face. The rope uncurled at a dizzying rate. The anchor bit into the rocky bottom. Her rope scudded against the brass hawse hole as momentum and inertia strained anchor, rope, and ship into a tight curl. *Fathom* skipped a bit, and it was hard to tell whether she was fighting the rope or she'd brushed her keel against a rock.

"Now!" bellowed Daniel. "Cut her now!"

William's blade made quick work of the three strands of nylon. The end still tied to the anchor shook away like a white snake diving deep. Harley sheeted the sails in.

They filled. *Fathom* heeled back over so she pierced her own wake back out into the wider part of the Funnel where she had come from. The wind picked up and bundled the fog away. The ocean was tidying her nasty toys for another day, another opponent less skilled than his grandfather.

"Oh, my God. Oh, my God," Harley jubilated. "Holy crap, Uncle Daniel, you … that …" But nothing could have said the current danger had passed more effectively than Daniel waving for Harley to drop her life jacket into a bench locker with his.

"Hold her on her present course, Harley," Daniel interrupted. His tone was sober. It reminded them there was a lot of ocean to negotiate. They were running parallel to the island, the long way to the ocean. Harley and William hoisted the main- and foresails.

Daniel turned the wheel this way and that. "Something's not right."

Harley agreed. "Yeah, she's sluggish. We damage the keel when we club hauled?"

"Maybe. It's in the stern."

Harley saw something flutter in their wake. "Someone's tied a bucket to the keel!"

William thought back to the Cape Islander and flipper splash he'd seen the day before. "I bet you it was Trenton!"

Daniel turned the schooner into the wind. "I'll have to dive and check it out. Get me the waterproof flashlight, will you please?"

“I’ve got my bathing suit on,” Harley said as she sprang from the hatchway, light in hand, peeling off her sweater and jeans and slipping her feet into a pair of flippers.

“William, tie the other end of this line to that stern cleat,” directed Daniel. Clutching the line, Harley held her mask and scissor-kicked into the cold Atlantic.

Daniel paced. Harley surfaced. She gulped air then dove again. Then she came back up with a bucket tied to a rope. Harley climbed the ladder clamped to the gunwale. Daniel comforted her. “Let’s get you some warm clothes and something warm to drink.”

“There’s a Thermos of hot chocolate in the hamper, Granddad,” explained William.

“Keep an eye out, will you, William?” said Daniel, closing the hatch behind them.

William grabbed the wheel in the waning darkness. The excitement of the impending race had delayed his sleep and the adrenalin rush he’d felt in the Funnel was wearing off. He leaned his tired head on the mast. McCoy appeared behind the sail and startled him.

“Why didn’t you help us?” challenged William in a hoarse whisper.

“I won’t always be here. Think back to the crash, William. Who helped you then?”

William forced his memory back to the submerged truck that haunted him.

“I remember hacking Dad’s seatbelt to get him out. Then having to float up to the air pocket and taking a last breath. I yelled, ‘Dad, you’re too big. I can’t get you out.’ When he didn’t move, I slid out the window. His eyes were open. I pulled myself onto the roof, pounding and yelling, ‘Dad! Dad! Get out, please. Dad!’ The waves knocked me off … and the tide pushed me to shore.”

The Real McCoy nodded. “You saved yourself, William.”

"I just left him there."

"Your dad's heart gave out before the crash. Nothing you could do. Nothing at all."

"When I see his eyes open like that, I wonder … did he suffer much?"

"Not nearly as much as you."

"But the water …"

"Dead before he hit it."

Dawn's light tore at the dark fabric. The Real McCoy faded.

"Granddad should see you. Settle your —"

McCoy held up his hand to stop him. "Concentrate on the race. I'll see you on the boat tonight afterwards. Concentrate!" McCoy faded as quickly as he had appeared.

The faint light played off his father's signature blue and red stitching. The hatchway slid open and Daniel emerged on deck followed by Harley, now dressed in warm clothes.

He started to take the helm but stopped long enough to run his hands under the edge of the binnacle that housed both the wheel and the compass. He found it. There was a magnet stuck in a piece of gum. "This is what threw off our compass." He tossed it below deck.

Daniel spread his legs for balance. "If we're done with Trenton's games, let's race."

Daniel turned the helm. Sea hungry, *Fathom* shook her sails loose, grabbed a belly full of wind, heeled over, and ran with poise for deep water.

Chapter Twenty-seven

The Race

Wing on wing: sails pushed on either side of the boat as it runs downwind

Fathom rounded the point. Deep in the harbour William saw the regatta of sailboats circling near the start. Each boat tried to get speed and position just right. With the binoculars he could see a nervous-looking Emmett and the Reverend Strawbridge in the Cape Island committee boat. Her motor idled as she rolled in the waves by the starting line buoys.

They could hear the radio announcer through speakers mounted on the committee boat foredeck. "Here we are, ladies and gentlemen, two minutes away from the start of another annual 'Old Classic Boat Race.' The old-timers who rejoiced at the news that Daniel McCoy was sailing won't be happy to hear he's not anywhere near the starting line. Oh, wait, there he is. But why is he so late in getting here?" Someone turned off the radio.

Harley looked grim as she glanced at her watch. She answered his puzzled look with, "We're a kilometre behind. We have to run outside those rocks all the way to the mouth of the harbour, then hurry all the way into the harbour just to get to the starting line." She anticipated his thoughts about just joining the race in progress. "The committee boat notes every boat that crosses the starting line. You don't do that, you're not considered in the race which will start long before we —"

BOOOM! The cannon barked the start of the race. Sails snapped as boats made for the starting line, with Trenton taking the early lead.

Fathom moved quickly along the length of black rocks. William shook his head at the thought that they'd cross the starting line well behind everyone else. Trenton hadn't sunk them, but had he created an insurmountable delay?

Harley pointed. "Look, Trenton's coming over to gloat."

Daniel flicked his chin to a marker just past the line of rocks. "Worse. He's going to force us away from the quickest route to get into the harbour. To delay us even more."

The smile Trenton gave Daniel from across the rocks had no humour and less warmth. He put his fingers to his head in a mock salute as a deckhand tailed lines.

William was alarmed. "Can he do that? Legally, I mean?"

"It's not sportsmanlike, but it's within the rules. He's the stand-on vessel so we have to give way. Damn. Half a boat length more and I'd risk it. But as it is, we'll have to circle around. All right, I'll fall off."

Wave Goodbye was off their port side and closing. Trenton nervously looked around. He didn't know the waters like Daniel did. That was a mistake. William cupped his hands and yelled, "RED RIGHT RUDDER RULE."

Trenton jerked his boat away. The channel between the rocks and Trenton widened.

"Belay that order. We're going to come about," shouted Daniel to Harley and William. "Ready about, helm's over."

Adrenalin and water surged. Daniel spun the helm hard over. Harley's eyes went wide as she and William slacked lines. *Fathom* ran ninety degrees to the oncoming *Wave Goodbye*. Trenton paled as *Fathom* appeared about to cut his boat in two.

At the last possible moment, Daniel threw the helm over and threaded *Fathom* between *Wave Goodbye* and the line of rocks. He ordered his crew to sheet the sails home. The sharp point of *Fathom*'s bowsprit raked over Trenton's stern, a hand's reach from where he stood in the cockpit. They never touched anyone or anything.

Harley yelped. "Wicked! Another coat of paint and we'd have hit 'em both."

Daniel kept his focus. The cousins grinned as they pulled in the sheets. *Fathom* ploughed into the harbour towards the committee boat and circled it smartly.

Emmett pumped his fist in triumph. The committee members murmured their doubts as *Fathom* flew past the starting line, finally in the race, but so far behind *Wave Goodbye*.

By the time they entered Mahone Bay the high sun had sailors stripping off jackets and grabbing sunscreen. The cheers from the crowd on Government Wharf grew louder as *Fathom* overtook a number of boats. They had cut Trenton's lead in half.

Wave Goodbye rounded a marker and was headed back towards them.

"I'm going to tell Trenton what I think of his cheating ways," Harley warned.

"No, you're not," answered Daniel. "We take the high road and focus on sailing."

Harley shook her head. But she would not argue with their captain. She busied herself coiling lines and sheets. William followed her example.

He looked up. They would pass very close to Trenton.

Daniel sensed his concern. "No worries. This time we're the stand-on vessel. We have the right of way on this tack. He has to give way and there's a lot of water here."

But it looked like Trenton wanted to test Daniel's nerve as he steered towards them.

Harley kept her head down as she recoiled a line just to stay busy. She was on the high side of the deck, the side Trenton would pass. At the last moment, Trenton's deckhand dropped two bumpers over the near side.

Without warning, Trenton jerked his helm over then back again. The stern of his boat banged her bumper into *Fathom* so hard that Harley lost her balance. She pitched right over the railing. Trenton laughed as he kept his course.

William leaned as far over the side as he could with his arm outstretched. He couldn't see Harley. She wasn't wearing a life jacket. There was that copper taste of fear again. She popped up in their wake like a cork, clutching the line she had been coiling.

"Don't come about," she screamed. "Just pull me in."

Daniel waved his agreement and said to William, "We'll have only one chance to get her in and quickly. If she tires she may not have the strength to stay above water."

Fighting panic, William pulled as hard as he could with Daniel, who only had one free hand for that task. Other boats had made the turn. They were coming too close to trust tying off the helm. *Fathom*'s forward momentum made it hard to pull Harley in. Daniel grabbed enough slack in the line to wrap around a winch. He released the winch handle from the leeside winch and clicked it in place.

William winched. Daniel tailed the line. He grabbed it with his left hand and moved it up to his teeth over and over till they had Harley right at their stern. Now Daniel risked slipping the tethering lines back over the helm's spindles. Together they pulled her over to the low side and back into the cockpit. Daniel took back the helm.

She sat, dripping and exhausted, then burst into nervous laughter. "What a jerk. He slowed us down, but he didn't stop us." She grinned in triumph.

"Ready about," called Daniel as they neared the race marker they had to circle.

Harley jumped up. They came about smartly and resumed their chase.

"Can he do that and get away with it?" blurted William.

"He was smart enough to do it with no witnesses about. It would be our word against his. Harley, well done, girl. Get yourself into some dry clothes."

Fathom continued to gain on other boats, passing them in twos and threes. Dingle actually cheered them as they overtook him.

Wave Goodbye was the last one to beat but she was still a half-kilometre away. Daniel scanned about. "Well, that's Little Duck Island and that, I think, is the race."

"But we're gaining on him at every marker," argued William.

Harley was sombre. "Just not enough time or ocean."

William pointed to the island. "Did you say that's Little Duck?" Daniel nodded. William turned ninety degrees and pointed to the peninsula. "Then the Gut is over there?" Daniel nodded, surprised he knew this. "We can sail through the Gut and make up for lost time."

"That would be cheating," said the skipper, inviting no further discussion on the issue.

Harley pointed to the near buoy. "The rule book says that once you've rounded the last buoy to starboard, you have to make it back to the finish line. Doesn't say you can't use the Gut." They scanned the narrow opening.

"Because only a fool would risk his boat through there," responded Daniel.

William looked to him. "Or a right good sailor." Daniel studied the rocky coast.

"Especially one who was racing for his house … and Emmett's boat," added Harley.

"Your father did it," said William.

"Well, there may be the devil to pay, but ready about. We're on a beam reach, so we'll be going 'wing on wing' with the main and the jib. Let's drop the foresail and go slowly."

Fathom came about and headed directly for the waterway, with the wind astern. William pulled her jib to port. Harley pushed the mainsail boom out to starboard.

On shore, the same woman called, "Vernon! Vernon! Come quick. They're back."

A scattering of people from the handful of houses dotting both sides of the Gut came out to watch the intrepid schooner running the gamut of shore rocks. Would she make it?

"Tide's going out." Daniel looked over the side at the water sluicing past. William added a warning, "Watch for mudbanks."

On cue *Fathom* lurched and skidded. The frail wind in her sails couldn't muscle her over the silt clinging to her keel. The spectators let out a collective, "Oh."

"Harley, take the helm." Daniel sprang from the controls. He clapped William on the back. "Follow me into the camber of the sail. Now!"

"What's Granddad doing?" William asked Harley.

"It's a fulcrum, or pivot, concept." She illustrated her point by holding her left forearm out perpendicular to the water. She walked two fingers of her right hand from the bent left elbow out to her left fist. It mimicked the added weight of two bodies that tilted up her left elbow. "With your combined weight as far out on the boom as possible, it tilts the keel. Hopefully just enough to free it."

Would it work? He followed Daniel to the base of the mast. Daniel climbed up onto the boom and shuffled along over the ocean. His back was against the camber or the belly of the sail. William froze before the mast.

Harley whispered encouragement: "The boat's in the water, you're not."

Daniel's foot slipped. He caught his balance and continued until his body lay in the pocket of the sail hanging way out over the water. He looked down to the keel. "Jack! Come on, Jack, we've done this before. I need your weight."

"I'm William, Granddad."

Daniel smiled at his time warp. "Right you are. Come on, William. Your father did it."

William looked at the safety line but decided against it.

"Take my hand, William," said Daniel, extending his out to him.

William leapt up into the sail. Daniel edged further back. His foot slipped again. This time he fell, clinging to the rigging beneath the boom, his back a few feet off the water.

William slithered to where Daniel hung. He extended his hand.

Daniel shook his head. "I'll just end up pulling you in."

"Harley, throw me the safety line you used for the bosun's chair."

Harley swung the spare line from the mast out to William. He tied a bowline around his middle. Harley caught the drift of his idea. She ran her end through a pulley and onto a winch. As he leaned forward she lowered his body to where Daniel could grab him.

As soon as Daniel clutched William, Harley cranked with a fury she didn't know she possessed. Inch by inch she pried them up. Both clung to each other's belts till they fell back into the camber of the sail.

Daniel pulled his grandson into a hug. *Fathom* heeled over just enough to pull forward in a sucking of mucky foam. They scrambled back to the deck.

The spectators cheered. Daniel clapped William on the back. "That was most impressive, William. Jack would be so proud of you." Daniel took the helm.

Harley punched William on the shoulder. "You did it, Will!"

Wave Goodbye emerged on the far side of the Gut. They saw Trenton stagger back. He must have believed he had won. But here they were on *Fathom* slicing from the narrow Gut and turning to parallel his course. *Fathom*'s sails filled on a reach.

Harley said under her breath, "No one can read the wind like Daniel can."

They could see committee members straining to watch the line between the two buoys. One of them trained his camera. Trenton's romp had turned to a photo finish.

Daniel leaned in to the two cousins. "Get ready to release the lines and sheet them home quickly. He's going to try to cut us off. Timing will make or break us."

As if he had heard his opponent, Trenton cut across Daniel's bow in an attempt to make him veer off.

At the last moment Daniel threw the sheet off the main. Wind spilled out of her and slowed just enough not to change course and let *Wave Goodbye* pass.

William felt as though time was standing still. He could hear the sails *whap*, *whap*, *whapping* above him. Water seemed to slow its friction along the hull. He became aware of the fact that he and Harley were hunched in tandem, waiting to put their backs into it, both of them panting. He felt the burning sensation from the ropes on his hands and the mitigating effect of the salt water. He could sense the heat from Harley's tanned arm against his. He was a regular on a great team.

"Pull that sheet. Pull for all you're worth!" bellowed his grandfather. They pulled the rope in, hand over hand, harnessing the wind. The crowd cheered. *Fathom* regained her speed. Her bowsprit cleared the finish line barely a metre ahead of *Wave Goodbye*.

Chapter Twenty-eight

Good Night

Binnacle: the post that houses the vessel's compass and sometimes also the wheel

The crowd on the dock whooped their delight. The cannon boomed the winner.

Fathom and *Wave Goodbye* sailed into the harbour, barely four metres apart.

Daniel eased his sails and she righted. William and Harley fell on the banquettes.

Trenton pulled abreast and shook his head in disbelief. "You, you McCoys. You manage to … you always …"

Harley tossed him the magnet he'd used to throw off the binnacle's compass.

William added softly, "Mr. Trenton, if you win, say little. If you lose, say less."

"Well, I'll tell you one thing. You'll never find McCoy's gold. If my father couldn't find it, you sure won't."

"It wasn't his to find, Mr. Trenton," said William. "And it wasn't your race to win."

Trenton couldn't answer. The weight of his defeat and treachery slumped him down on the banquette. His crewman spun them away from the harbour's cheering masses.

The second wave of applause washed over the winning boat. Emmett brought the committee boat alongside. Reverend Strawbridge handed Daniel the sailing trophy. William touched the silver band with his father's name on it. Grandfather and grandson exchanged a smile.

Emmett gave his cousin a bear hug. "You sweet, righteous, hell-raising reprobate. You have more nerve than a toothache." Then he realized what he'd said in front of Reverend Strawbridge. "Sorry, Reverend, I just —"

"No, no, Emmett, you're right. He is a sweet, righteous … reprobate."

Harley gave her cousin a bear hug. "Thanks for, for saving the loft and everything."

Daniel gestured to a nasty scrape Harley had taken when she fell overboard. "You best get that tended to."

"Let's all go ashore and have a pint at the Taffrail," invited Emmett.

William was worried he wouldn't make his meeting with McCoy. Daniel saved him. "Actually, Emmett, I'd like to get back and see Mary. Her husband hasn't been around much of late. We'll be there for tomorrow's big dockside lunch and presentation."

Harley jumped aboard the committee boat. Daniel, the quiet warrior, waved to the applauding crowd. He nodded his thanks for their support before sailing home.

The spokes on *Fathom's* helm were tethered to keep her on course. William and Daniel stood together in her foredeck's faint moonlight. Daniel's house rose in the distance. The wind was light but steady, as if tired from the day's efforts and emotions.

The wooden boat creaked. Daniel shot a glance up the mast.

"He really did leave me a beauty of a schooner, didn't he? A real winner?" He cleared his chest of a decades-old weight when he said, "I was afraid. That telegram he sent me in 1947? The one that said he was coming? I was afraid ... to meet him. He was a father I'd longed to meet for so long. Then they said he killed Cavendish. A hero and a killer all wrapped up in one. I think you and Jack are right. He wasn't the kind of man to kill someone. And I never gave him a chance to explain because I panicked. Something you didn't do today when we were stuck on the mudbanks." He gave William a sidelong smile.

"You don't look frightened when you sail, Granddad."

"Never afraid when I sail. Got that from my father too."

A wistful look came over Daniel. He leaned into her stays. "He left me this beauty. It was all the affection time allowed him." He looked to the sky and said, "Thanks for caring when you could."

Where was the Real McCoy? Why was he taking so long to show up now that Daniel was willing to make up? What if he didn't show up at all?

William rubbed his hands together nervously. Daniel misread it as William being chilled. "I'll go below and get some food to warm us up. Mary gave us a Thermos of soup. Keep an eye open for any hazards," he said, flicking his index to the bow that pushed further into the night's darkness.

William sighed. McCoy materialized beside him.

"You took your time."

McCoy winked at him. "After all these years of yearning to be set free, I indulged a few more minutes — my last aboard this grand, floating prison." He patted the mast in a goodbye gesture. He ran his finger in the furrow dug by Cavendish's bullet — so much history.

William untied the rigging knife. "I've got something of yours."

"You keep it. You'll have more use for it now. Nice race today. I'm glad to see you're not afraid of the water anymore, William."

William nodded.

"Thanks for setting me free." McCoy started to fade.

William reached out to his waning image. "Wait!"

"It doesn't work that way. Even pain and sorrow have a limited life."

"But Granddad needs to see you!" cried William.

"No. I needed him to understand that — how did he put it, I cared when I could. He's at peace with who I was. Now I can be too."

"Hey, what about our deal?" asked William. "What did you hide for Granddad?"

"You're standing on it — as sure as your father was his father's son. And you yours."

The Real McCoy's image grew even fainter.

"Tell my father …," started William.

The Real McCoy looked at him intently.

"I miss him," blurted William.

"He knows."

"Tell him I'm sorry I didn't pull him out … even if it was too late."

"He knows. Farewell. Fair wind." The Real McCoy was gone.

William had so many questions. What had he meant with his message, *Keelhaul*?

Daniel came up the hatchway with two mugs of steaming soup. William wove his way back to the cockpit with the rolling gait of an old salt.

Daniel put the mugs down and hugged William. And William, in turn, wrapped his arms firmly around his grandfather, who gave William the triple-pat his father had given him.

"You and me, finding ourselves after all this time … is quite a haul. Quite a haul," said Daniel with a smile.

William's mouth dropped open. "It is a haul. It's … Keelhaul, keelhaul. I think I've figured out the riddle. We have to pull *Fathom* out of the water. Right now, Granddad. Right now."

They pressed her home through the Funnel.

A few minutes later, William and his grandfather dropped *Fathom*'s sails. They snugged her up into the boat cradle; Harley had winched down the rails for them.

"Okay, Harley!" yelled William. "Pull us in."

The winch motor started up. The cable inched forward. Then a crack sounded in the night and the cradle listed slightly to starboard and stopped.

Grinding metal shrieked louder than a flock of seagulls. Smoke billowed out of the winch housing. Harley turned it off and shrugged.

William bolted down the hatchway. He came back up pulling on the mask and flippers Harley had used. With the flashlight in hand, he leapt off the deck with a splash and disappeared. He surfaced a moment later and called out, "One of the wheels on the cradle snapped."

"Will," Harley said, smiling, "you're swimming." He smiled and climbed back aboard.

Emmett yelled, "The motor's not strong enough. She'll blow a bearing."

"Uncle Emmett, we need the tractor. Please," shouted William. He tied a line off the bow and threw it to shore.

From up the hill came the roar of the tractor. Emmett was partway down the hill when the motor sputtered to a stop. Emmett threw his arms up in a gesture of resignation. "She's out of fuel." He jumped off. Mary left the veranda and walked down with him.

Harley hurried to the water's edge. "Sorry, Will. There's nothing strong enough to help the winch overcome that stupid broken wheel."

William scanned the schooner. He studied the telltales on the stays. "Granddad, there's an onshore breeze blowing, right?"

"A good one, yes," said Daniel, not sure where William was going with all of this.

"Then we do have something strong enough: the wind and my father's sails." He patted his father's blue and red stitching for luck.

Daniel watched him hoist the main. Realizing what he was about, he helped lay out as much sail as possible.

"Start the winch, Harley," William yelled over his shoulder. Harley put it in gear. The boat didn't move and the winch let out another cry of protest. The wind picked up. The sails stretched full out in support of William's idea.

The power of the sails allowed the cradle to limp onto to dry land. Harley killed the winch. She tromped over to Mary and Emmett, who stood watching from shore. William and Daniel lowered the sails. William dropped to the wet sand glinting in the tractor's headlights.

He crouched by a gash in *Fathom*'s keel. "Here! Look at this. I was right, Granddad." They gathered around the keel where it had hit the ocean floor. A strip of gold shone in the gash. McCoy's gold had been melted down and hidden in the keel.

"We must have cut the keel on a rock in the Funnel or the Gut," explained William. "It was a riddle. He didn't mean *Keelhaul* as in 'he should be keelhauled.' He wanted to tell you the 'haul' was in the keel."

Harley added, "It went up and down and was hidden six feet deep."

Daniel draped an arm around Mary's shoulders. "*Fathom*! He wanted me to figure out that he'd hidden the gold six feet below deck in the keel."

William nodded. "That's why he wouldn't let you sell it."

With the tip of his knife, Emmett peeled back thin strips of wood. McCoy had fitted his melted gold into the keel. Emmett marvelled, "My God, I've never seen so much gold."

William looked at Emmett and asked, "Do you think it's worth as much as Dingle's bank loan for Dad's sail loft?"

Emmett shook his head no. "No, sir. No, sir, it's worth more. A lot more than he needs to pay back the loan."

"So we won't need Trenton's mortgage," marvelled Mary.

"Daniel, what are you going to do with all this?" asked Emmett.

Daniel looked to Mary, then to William. "Well, the first thing we're going to do is spruce up William's bedroom."

William, Mary, Emmett, and Harley stared at Daniel.

"Well, it's not really geared up for him to move into — during the summer months. And holidays, if he wants to come. Should be a good place for a young man to come to if he wants to apprentice in the sailmaking business."

Everyone was quiet.

"And, if we did that, your mother might like to come more often. We would want your mother to feel welcome here, William. Wouldn't we? We should call in the morning and ask her what she thinks."

William grinned at Harley. "Shall we have some … hot chocolate?"

They burst into Daniel's kitchen in a fit of nervous laughter, no one really able to take in the fact that they had found the phantom's gold.

Emmett passed the bottle of rum they'd found to Daniel. He held it aloft and looked to his grandson. "Here's to Jack McCoy … who made sails as strong as his son."

Emmett and Harley joined in with a hearty, "Hear, hear!"

His grandmother had her arms around his grandfather's left arm and leaned on it. She smiled to William as she wiped away a tear of happiness.

William thought back to his father's words about his mother, the ones he'd read in his father's diary. He thought back to his father's sail loft. He was maybe eight, wearing the sou'wester, standing on a chair in front of an old ship's wheel on a binnacle his father had bolted to the floor. His father stood behind him. Both sang "Down by the Bay." They pretended to sail in heavy weather as rain beat on the windows.

He remembered his father draping an arm over his shoulder. He recalled his father's advice as he did homework in the loft on weekends and Wednesdays before Scrabble dinners at the pub. He remembered the man who had laughed as they'd driven to Lunenburg. They had come for William's first race on that fateful trip with the man who had loved him as best he could for as long as he could. It wasn't all the affection that William had wanted. It was all the affection time had allowed his father.

He looked up at the ceiling.

"I'll be back in a while." He patted his grandmother's shoulder as he sprang from the room.

The moon had risen above the treetops and bathed the highway in a soft light. William brought his bike to a stop a few miles from his grandparents' house. This was where the pickup had left the road and plunged into the ocean, where his father had died.

William dropped his bike by the side of the road. He looked out into the darkness. Waves *clickety-clacked* the stones up and down. He no longer hated or feared the ocean. He opened the box he had tied to his carrier and gently removed its contents.

He kicked off his sandals and rolled his pant legs. He waded in and placed his father's model sailing dinghy on the water. "Thanks for caring all the times you could."

The model's sails filled. She pulled away from shore. He triple-patted the ocean and said, "Good night, Dad, I love you."

A flow of emotion rippled the surface of this big, impartial body of water.

Postscript

Writing *The Phantom's Gold* has been a labour of love that involved extensive historical research. All of the characters are fictional except for William (Bill) McCoy, a.k.a. the Real McCoy. I hope my fictional account of his ghost does honour to this individual described as "a straight man in a crooked world."

To the best of my knowledge McCoy was born in upper New York State, was married and divorced, did not have any children, and owned a boatyard in Florida. When the economy soured he and his brother pooled their resources to buy the schooner *Arethusa* in Gloucester, Massachusetts, and used it as a rum-runner.

McCoy used the ports of Saint-Pierre, the Bahamas, Halifax, and Lunenburg, among others. In Saint-Pierre he used the normal loading docks. The floating shed is fictional. When he retired from rum-running, McCoy bought a Tancook schooner and turned her into a pleasure craft in 1935. He is purported to have said he'd return as a ghost to warn people against the excesses of alcohol.

The Corkum mentioned in *The Phantom's Gold* is not Chief Corkum of Lunenburg. Corkum had left the police to work as a tax collector for two years before returning to the police.

A number of books are available to those interested in the rum-running trade, including *On Both Sides of the Law* by Hugh Corkum, *Moonshiners, Bootleggers & Rumrunners* by Derek Nelson, and, possibly the definitive book on McCoy, *The Real McCoy* by Frederick F. Van de Water. It has been republished by Flat Hammock Press.

For information on Tancook schooners one can read *The Tancook Schooners: An Island ands its Boats* by Wayne M. O'Leary.

Those interested in the storied career of the famous *Bluenose* should read *A Race for Real Sailors* by Keith McLaren.

Bluenose Ghosts will give the reader a good account of Maritime ghosts.

Music lyrics in *The Phantom's Gold* are by Lowry Olafson.

Glossary

Ahoy: a sailor's call to attract attention, akin to hello
Banquette: a long bench in a sailboat's cockpit
Beam: the side of the vessel
Beam reach: the point of sail where the vessel is at right angle to the wind
Belay: an order to cease an action or previous order
Belaying pin: a pin made of wood or steel that secures a line; releasing the pin releases the line
Bilge: the lowest part of vessel, designed to collect water to be released
Binnacle: the post that houses the vessel's compass and sometimes also the wheel
Bluenose: a famous Canadian fishing schooner that won numerous sailing prizes
Boatswain: a.k.a. bosun, a non-commissioned officer in charge of sails and ropes
Bollard: substantial pillar to which the boat is secured, usually dockside
Boom: the horizontal spar to which the foot of the sail is secured
Bosun: pronunciation of "boatswain," a non-commissioned officer in charge of rigging
Bosun's chair: a planked or strapped seat to hoist a sailor working on rigging
Bow: the front of the vessel
Bowline: a knot that is easy to do, won't slip, and is easy to undo if not under stress

Bowsprit: a spar extending from the bow to secure foremast and foresail (jib)
Broach: to be thrown sideways down the trough or face of a large wave
Camber of the sail: a pocket created by wind
Cape Islander: a fishing motor trawler designed in the early 1900s, strong and reliable
Cat-o'-nine-tails: a nine-tailed whip used by the navy for discipline
Chart: a map of the sea surface used for navigation
Chart table: a below-deck table used to roll out a chart
Cleat: a stationary object that allows a line to be secured on a vessel
Clew: the end of a sail by the outermost point on a boom
Club haul: a technique for quickly turning a sailboat by spinning it on its anchor
Coaming: the raised edge of a cockpit or hatch that keeps water out
Cockpit: the steering area nearer the stern of a smaller vessel
Come about: changing direction so as to sail at the same angle but with the wind on the other side; tacking
Cowling: the cover of a motor
Cutter: a boat carrying pilots or law enforcement officials
Dacron: synthetic material used for sails
Davits: horizontal spars that allow a boat to be lowered over the side or stern
Deckhand: a sailor who works on deck
Drogue: a conical sea anchor used to slow a boat down in a storm
Eddy: movement of water that doubles back on itself like a whirlpool
Fathom: a measure of six feet; also means to understand
Founder: to take on water and sink
Furl: to roll or gather a sail against the mast or, more usually, the boom
Galley: a ship's cooking area
Gaff hook: a hook on a long pole used to gather fish
Gimballed: a mechanism that allows a stove to sway in harmony with a boat's movement

Gunwale: the raised sides of a boat once used for guns, hence "gun wall"
Hatchway: the covered passageway below deck
Hawse: a hole in side of a ship through which the anchor chain or a rope can pass
Head: a ship's lavatory
Heave-to: to adjust course to slow or stop a vessel
Heeling: the angle a ship leans under pressure from the wind
Helm: a vessel's steerage
Helm's down: helm has been turned, and the vessel is changing course
Highliner: the dory fisherman who caught the most fish and got the biggest share of the sale; a successful man
Jib: a small rectangular foresail
Keelhaul: to drag a person beneath the keel as punishment
Lanyard: a rope or small line that ties something off
Leeward: the direction the wind is going (as opposed to coming from: windward)
Line: the proper term for most "ropes" on a ship
Luff: the flapping of a sail when it is no longer filled with wind or optimally used
Marlinspike: a tool used to separate strands of a rope or undo screw pins
Mast: a vertical spar to support sails or rigging
Masthead: the top of the mast
Mooring: a place or line that holds a vessel in place
Painter: the bow line used to tow or secure a tender
Pennant: a thin, triangular flag flown from the masthead
Petty officer: a non-commissioned officer, from the French, *petit*
Port: where ships unload, often in a harbour
Rails: part of the lifelines that keep sailors from falling overboard
Ready about: a call to indicate a change of course or tack
Refitting: maintenance and upkeep of a boat

Rigging: the ensemble of lines and masts that support a boat's sails
Rigging knife: a knife used in managing lines
Rum-runner: someone who smuggles alcohol
Running lights: lights needed for a boat sailing at night
Sail loft: a loft or rooms where sails are cut and sewn together
Schooner: a sailing vessel with at least two masts, with the foremast being smaller
Sextant: a navigational tool that determines bearings by using sun and stars
Shackle: a metal fastener of different sizes secured with a pin screwed in place
Sheet: a rope used to set a sail in proportion to the wind
Sheet home: tighten up a sail till it is flat for more efficiency and power
Sling lead: throw the sounding lead to determine depth, also called sounding
Sloop: single-masted sailboat
Sou'wester: wide-brimmed, waterproof hat used during storms
Spinnaker: a large sail used to sail downwind
Spindle: slender pegs on a boat's wheel
Spindrift: water particles blown from the top of a wave
Spreaders: a spar that pushes the shrouds out for greater effectiveness
Stanchion: a vertical post on a deck that supports the lifeline
Stays: rigging running from a mast to the deck
Starboard: the right side of a boat
Stern: the back of a vessel
Storm jib: smaller jib used during a storm
Tack: to change the direction a boat sails into the wind — starboard and port tack
Taffrail: the rail at the stern of a boat
Tail a line: to coil a line that is being pulled in
Tancook schooner: a schooner designed and made in Tancook Island, N.S.

Telltale: a light string attached to the rigging to determine wind direction and strength

Tender: a small boat that services a larger boat at mooring or dock

Transom: the flat surface at the stern of a boat

Trim the sails: make them more efficient

Windward: the direction the wind is coming from

Wing on wing: sails pushed on either side of a boat as it runs downwind

Acknowledgements

Most writers work in isolation, but many others are relied upon to get us to and from that island and sustain us while we're there. At the beginning there was Nika Rylski, everyone's favourite structure martinet. Sean Chercover told me I was a writer when I most needed to hear it. Will O'Hara, Tom Dutton, and Paul Sinel are my Iron Men — may we never rust. Thomas Walden, Eric Birnberg, Jamie Paul Rock, and Anne Frank saw the book's potential as a film.

In Halifax there was Verity Leach and Chris Fyles, without whose generous hospitality I could not have done my research. Chris Reardon, photographer extraordinaire, knows everyone in Nova Scotia and shares that knowledge. While any nautical errors are my own, Walter Flowers showed me the Gut, and Tom Gallant, raconteur and bluewater sailor, introduced me to his Tancook schooner, *The Avenger*.

The gang at the Humber School for Writers included Frieda Wishinsky and Marianne Fedunkiw. Carl Harvey, Barbara Berson, Marian Hebb, Dom Fiore, and Jack Grin steadied my course.

My publishers, Marc Coté and Barry Jowett, provided insight and gentle guidance and, most importantly, they believed.

Last but far from least there's Clarinda, who taught me that the term "long haul" could be so sexy; Julien, who showed me what being a hero was all about; and Liliana, who puts so much lustre in the word "brilliant."

This book is dedicated to Leo Murphy, who fought during the Second

World War with DEMS (Defensively Equipped Merchant Ships) and who bought us our first sailboat, a thirteen-foot sailing dinghy, and taught us to harness the wind and not fear it.